I Will Wait for You...

A Saga of Forbidden Love

Ranjeet Singh

PEACOCK BOOKS

DISCLAIMER

All the characters in this novel have no existence outside the imagination of the author, and have no relation whatsoever to anyone bearing the same name or names. They are not even distantly inspired by any individual known or unknown to the author, and all the incidents are pure invention.

Published by
PEACOCK BOOKS
7/22, Ansari Road, Darya Ganj,
New Delhi-110002
Phones : +91-11-40775252, 23273880, 23275880, 23280451
Fax : +91-11-23285873
Web : www.atlanticbooks.com
E-mail : orders@atlanticbooks.com

Branch Office
5, Nallathambi Street, Wallajah Road,
Chennai-600002
Phones : +91-44-64611085, 32413319
E-mail : chennai@atlanticbooks.com

*Peacock Books is an imprint of
Atlantic Publishers and Distributors (P) Ltd*

ISBN 978-81-248-0253-3

Printed in India at Nice Printing Press, A-33/3A, Site-IV, Industrial Area, Sahibabad, Ghaziabad, U.P.

Dedicated to

My dear Ruchi
Who made a difference in my life

Preface

The story begins with the appointment of a teacher in a school. He finds an atmosphere of warmth and geniality among the students and a congenial working environment. Life runs smoothly until he falls in passionate love with a beautiful lady teacher.

The story gets serious when one night, he dreams of a nightmare that sends a chill down his spine and cuddles his blood. He finds the situation frightening, unpleasant and difficult to deal with. Some strange and mysterious happenings like car accident, encounter with a shadow, a few deaths and some other mishaps start taking place. But somehow he survives and tackles the situation with the assistance of his favourite students and his love.

The mystery of shadow gets revealed at last when he encounters the truth of his previous life. Ultimately, he escapes the nasty state of affairs with the help of the Exorcist and the Principal. Finally, he leaves the school with bitter-sweet memories of some lovely faces.

Ranjeet Singh

Acknowledgements

This exciting, enjoyable and a thrilling experience has been possible with the kind assistance of my dear friends. I therefore, express my heartfelt thanks and sense of gratitude to—Ruchi, Preeti, Reeta, Ankita, Sagun, and Archana—who have given their help and moral support during last few years.

I would also like to thank Sunbeam Family that offered me a hand to come with them when I was lagging behind.

Last but not least, I am thankful to Dr. K.R. Gupta, Honorary Advisor and Mr. Harjeet Singh Publishing Co-ordinator of Atlantic Publishers and Distributors (P) Ltd. for the interest evinced in publishing this book.

Ranjeet Singh

Contents

CHAPTER ONE

The Hiss of Moonless Night

The cool wind had chilled me to the bone when I reached the campus on a Sunday evening. The gatekeeper opened the gate; picked up my luggage and made me sit in his small room. A small fire was burning to take the chill off the room. He gave a call; reported my arrival and enquired of my lodging. Meanwhile I relieved myself feeling warm and cozy sitting beside the bonfire.

He requested a Macabre, who was also sitting around fire, to carry my luggage. The man in rags exhibited clumsy movements and stared back.

"It's blood chilling cold outside. I'll not stir out." The Macabre denied abruptly.

The gatekeeper appeared strained and a little unnerved.

"Don't worry, sir, I'll arrange someone quickly." He suggested politely.

I was quite desperate to find my lodging and take rest. My back and leg muscles had been aching since the long ride from Bareilly to Shimla had tired me out. In a couple of minutes, an aged Hillbilly reached there. He had bags under his red-rimmed eyes and deep, craggy wrinkles down his cheeks. His skin was so pale and dried out, no color at all, as if he had been sick for a long time. His long white hair looked as if it hadn't been brushed since weeks! He murmured; gave a strange gaze; picked up my luggage; asked to follow him.

The campus, surrounded by majestic mountains, was full of invigorating pure air and greens. The hissing sound of the wind was crooning in my auditory senses. The trees were swaying in the wind. The beautiful, sequestered and tranquil sight was very similar to the painted dream on a piece of paper. In brief, the relaxed ambience of the school was Nature's blessings upon the earth.

The hills around were shrouded in mist. The campus was fully covered in a thick blanket of fog hampering the visibility. The patches of dense fog were striking against the face. My eyes had grown misty and ears ice-cold.

It was a well-known Boarding School named St. Andrews Convent Public School in Shimla, the Queen of Hill stations, situated in the foothills of the Himalaya ranges. The school building was styled in tudorbethan and neo-gothic architecture dating from the colonial era. It offered a haven of peace and serenity away from the bustle of the city.

I thanked God when we reached a huge building. The old man started climbing the flight of stairs. My backpack bounced on my shoulders as I climbed. My heart was coming to my mouth at every step. I was carrying myself staggering after him. He took a round of the building at the II floor and led me in a room through a corridor. He unlocked the gate and dumped my luggage inside.

"This is your room sir." he said in a shivering voice.

"Thank you very much". I nodded gratefully.

When he backed away, his chin was quivering, and his pale gray eyes were wet. The extremely unpleasant and frightening figure disappeared into thin air.

The walls gave some protection from the prevailing cool wind. It was a well furnished bright and sparkly room with attached washroom. Long queen-sized bed, cupboard, sofa and a big table cheered me up. Over all, the room was so strangely beautiful that I could only describe it as 'magical'.

I felt ready to drop so I let my luggage rest for some time and threw myself on the bed. The gate was left open, but I was unmindful to all this and was relaxing myself closing my eyes. The moments of respite got disturbed when I heard a great uproar nearby. I put fingers in my ears and felt disinterested, but the noise kept on getting louder and louder. I took the pillow and covered my right ear tightly. Still the awful din was striking my auditory senses. I felt crossed; got up; the eyes were still closed; feeling to attack the nuisance causing people like Don Quixote. My head felt ready to explode.

"What's all this mess? Here the people can't have even a few minutes rest full of serene and tranquility" I was annoyed at myself.

I again fell down in bed. I was rolling; changing the sides; shifting the positions of the pillow. But nothing worked out. When I could not control, I came out of the gate of my room. There I encountered a catch-22 situation—two students fighting, and rest of them uttering high-pitched giggles.

On the same floor at a distance, there was Boys Hostel.

In a flash, a blooming Princess of sweet 20 came on the screen brandishing a thick stick in her hands. I had an outstanding view of her unflawed back and long legs, wondering how beautiful she was!

"Why are you shouting, fighting and disturbing? Don't you have the sense that teachers are taking rest?" She shouted and caned a boy standing there.

I pulled myself inside the room so that the lady might not see me and feel awkward.

"Where is your warden? Let him come. I'll complain against you all today." She kept on shouting.

The boys had torn the clothes of each other so they were standing in half naked state.

"Don't you have shame to stand naked like this before a lady teacher (indicating the torn lower of the student)? Go and change your clothes" she roared.

The boy looked downward and got to know that his inner organs were coming out. Feeling embarrassed, he looked for coverage. He suddenly snatched the pink colored stall covering breasts from shoulders of the lady and rushed wrapping his waist downstairs. The students enjoyed the scene and whooped it up. The lady was stunned for a while and felt blushed. She didn't shout, just glared at me silently, and then gave a close chase to the boy in the same direction. The scene was too amusing to keep myself indoors. I stepped out in corridor and entertained myself seeing the sizzling beauty chasing the tiny Imp. I felt the moonlight going with the sizzling beauty.

"Thank God! The ultimate drama is finally over" I whispered squeezing my hands against my head.

I retreated and bumped into my bed in the dark. The knees were hurt, but the heart amused. I therefore, preferred laughing that made me forget my pain.

The gate was still open; the students were moving in the corridor; perchance they were going to have dinner. Realization dawned upon me that 'these imps are the neighbors of the resident teachers'. I was confounded to imagine all time disturbances at the gate.

I collected myself; got out of bed; took a hasty shower; put on nightclothes; and settled down on bed. I felt the tumult of the corridor entering inside me. The imp rats were playing *kabaddi* in my stomach. I approached the Intercom; looked for Campus Phone Directory and asked the Mess-In-Charge to arrange my dinner in my room.

Meanwhile, I preferred arranging my luggage; a few books on the table; clothes in the cupboard. It was almost 9 o'clock at night when the door bell rang.

I stepped towards the door; unbolted and opened it with pulsating heart. I heard the dishes rattling and dinner smelt delicious. A flicker of smile ran on my face.

A small boy with tray in his hands entered and placed it on the table.

"Do you want anything else, Sir?" He asked in a most humble way.

"No thanks. This is enough." I replied.

The boy made a quick exit.

I relished the pleasant dinner; washed hands and went to bed. It being a daily practice, I took out my book and comforted myself with a pillow on snug bed. The mind being obsessed with the day experiences was incapable to let me access the book. I tried my best, but it didn't work. My body was also aching and crying for rest. I ended the struggle; took the pillow lying on a side; lay down with the book in my arms pressing it close to my heart.

The leaden eyelids brought a day full of happenings to a close. The sweet memories of the cute face reflected. The face of the charming Princess who came like lightning and went like thunder was still fresh somewhere in the subconscious mind. She looked stunningly beautiful that moment. The pleasing figure wearing tight fitting Jeans, a pretty top of latest formal cut, tinkling ear rings, red paste on her lips and shining lovely rose colored face with a cute killing smile was looking at me with a stick in her hands. I got scared and opened my eyes. She was no more there, but every skill of her figure was tickling me. Some kind of spell was overcoming me. I wanted to tell her not to rob me of my sleep. I remained lying in bed, and the sleep crept on me at an unknown hour.

CHAPTER TWO

The Pinks and Yellows of the Sunrise

I woke up with the noises in the corridor in the morning. But the noises were not cacophonous like the previous evening. Opening the gate I saw, the students were going for the morning walk and warm up exercise. They were running here and there in the corridor for their shoes and tracksuits. I banged the door loudly, and crept into bed once more to enjoy the morning sleep. Soon I received an invitation from sweet sleep and I pressed it close to my heart.

When I woke up, I could smell a sweet scent in my room. Living here was very different from home and quite an experience. It was seven o'clock. Outside my window, golden beams of sunlight shot through the tall, snow covered pines.

"It's so pretty and uncluttered here." I murmured softly spreading myself.

Soon, I climbed out of bed with a smile on my face; brushed my teeth; refreshed myself and started getting ready for the school.

I dressed myself in formals; brushed my hair studying my face in the mirror. I felt a growing sense of alarm perceiving a fresh bloomed rose placed there.

"How can a flower reach here?" I pondered.

"I knew full well that flowers don't walk their own." I joked apart.

"It might be the mischief of the students, and a way to welcome the new teacher." I kept talking to myself.

When I didn't get any sign or clue, I shrugged the issue aside...I was getting late for the school so I locked my room and headed towards Academic Block to cope with the challenges of boarding school.

Annexed to the Resident staff accommodation, houses included study-bedrooms or dormitories, a dining room or refectory where boarders took meals at fixed times, and a library, hall or cubicles where they could do their homework. Houses also had common rooms for television and relaxation, kitchens for snacks, and perhaps computer, ping-pong or billiards rooms. There were abundant shaded outside areas for conversation and tranquil reflection.

On my way to dining hall, I again met the scene that reminded me of the last night's episode. A young man in his twenties was waving a stick and terrifying the students on the ground floor. He wore a brown sheepskin jacket, open to reveal a blue-and-white sky sweater pulled down over baggy jeans.

Now, I was well familiar that 'naughtiness is mixed in their bones and it is a great challenge to tackle them'.

I placed myself directly in his line of sight. Suddenly, the guy turned and caught sight of me. He was a sorry sight, soaked to the skin and felt awkward.

"Get back to your classes" he shouted at the students.

"I don't want any noise again." He shouted further.

The students retreated to their classrooms and he gave me a broad smile. The guy was genial, strict in discipline, dutiful and well built.

"Good Morning, sir!" he spoke loudly and impressively walking towards me, "No one is sorrier than I am about what happened.... Bye the way, I am Abhishek appointed as PTI here." Shaking hand with me he blabbered.

"I'm Tanmay." I introduced and returned his smile with all courtesy, "By the way, it's a nice way of handling the students with sticks." I taunted. "School discipline plays a key of a successful life but it must be inculcated not forced." I reposted.

"Oh Sir, you are new here so you don't know how naughty they are!" He justified, "We can't administer these Imps without sticks." He continued. "Don't worry—you'll soon get used to this sense of stick." He said with a naughty smile.

"I don't think I can ever get used to apply coercion power living with these blooming buds." I gave serious consideration to the matter.

"Well I'm ready to do some serious eating. Abhi, would you mind accompanying me for breakfast?" I asked warmly. "I'm afraid I'm not a very serious person" I exclaimed.

"I don't have mind to mind such things." He exhibited the rare flash of humor of his own brand. He thought it best to humor us rather than get into an argument. The scene was hilarious—we couldn't stop laughing.

By the time we had reached the dining hall. It was very spacious and gave a congenial look. It was quite neat and clean to place a high importance on hygiene. The food and snacks served to the students were well balanced and nutritious, promoting health awareness rather than promotion of junk food consumption. Though there were separate Halls for boys and girls yet the breaks for recess were staggered so that at one point there were only a limited number of students.

All of a sudden, we heard a thud sound and a loud cry nearby. We set off at a smart pace. We saw a small boy lying on the floor and weeping bitterly.

"Good morning teachers!" The boys who were taking their breakfast stood up instantly.

"Good morning!" I responded.

"Sit down and finish your breakfast." Shouldering to the small boy's cry on, I said.

There was every cause for concern so I turned to students and inquired into the matter. A senior student stood up for the small boy, and reported me with all reverence.

"Actually sir, the students are served four breads in the breakfast. If they need more, they have to request the Head Cook. If he's merciful, he gives one or two more, but never more than two. On the other hand, if he is cross, he can deny; show his anger or even snatch the plate forcefully." He took a pause; lifted the glass from the table; drank the water and resumed.

"Sorry sir…Actually today the boy had already taken his share, but he wanted more. The Head Cook was not here to serve. He might be a bit hungrier so he himself took four slices extra. The Head Cook noticed him taking extra slices. He came rushing; snatched the plate with a jerk. Consequently, the boy couldn't bear the jerk and fell down." The senior boy finished the story.

I saw the seraphic little boy still gazing hungrily at the display of food. He had stopped sobbing. He squinted at me and burst out with a sob, "Sir, he always does so. It's his daily routine. Whenever I ask for more, he takes out his frustration on me." he uttered with tears rolling down his eyes.

His tears seemed to grieve a kind hearted man like me. I took out my handkerchief and began to wipe his tears.

I thought the things stood at present over before jumping to conclusion. I couldn't tolerate all this so I took the Head Cook to task, "Mr. Cook, don't you know how to behave with these students? They are like your sons and daughters. If they ask for little more, what's bad in that? Their parents have paid for their food. You are not running orphanage here." I scolded him.

"Sir, we are given a limited supply of breads. We have to manage in that quantity only," he justified, "Today, I was really at fault. I should not have snatched the plate. I beg your pardon sir." He spoke with pleading eyes.

"Next time, you won't find any such mistake." He promised.

The boy was happy to see the Head Cook being scolded and feeling sorry. He finished his breakfast happily. The students started moving out.

I was lost brooding then I felt a hand around my waist and a voice.

"I'm afraid you are really a serious person. Take my Mantra and discard your mind to mind." Abhishek joked apart.

"All this talk of food is making me hungry." He again flashed the humor of his own brand.

His eyes had a wild hungry look in them so I preferred breakfast over all these nasty affairs. Abhi indicated to the breakfast that had already been served.

"God is so unfair with these small kids." I murmured, pouring maple syrup over the toast.

Abhi nodded and smiled; smiled and nodded; then burst out laughing.

"Abhi, be serious yaar." I suggested him gravely.

He laughed all the more loudly. His laughter tickled me and I also joined him.

Meanwhile, that small boy came bouncing; stood by my side. "Sir, stoop down your head." he whispered lovingly. Taking him seriously, I stooped my head to his side. He caught my head between his tiny soft hands; kissed my left cheek and ran away saying, "thank you sir." I felt rejoiced to see the small boy bouncing.

We moved to the Academic Block. There was a very beautiful open space on the three sides of the two-storey school building surrounded by Lawns, landscaped garden and playground. The buildings had been designed to blend in with their surroundings. The aesthetically designed garden was designated an area of outstanding natural beauty all around. Then I heard my name being addressed in a manly voice.

"Hello Tanmay! Good morning!" The Principal Mr. Peter Drummond wished me with a smile. His smile was as faded as he was old in years. He was standing at a distance and addressing a few employees who I thought were supervising the construction work.

Though quite old, he had an impressive personality and dominating demeanor. His very appearance or voice was enough to arouse panic and consternation in the students.

"Hello! Tanmay, how are you?" he asked in glee and tried to appeal to my finer feelings.

"It's my finest hour and a great honour to be invited here." I answered respectfully.

"How did you like your accommodation?" He asked further. "It's really nice; quite comfortable." I thanked him.

"Look! This is your schedule of the classes." Handing over a sheet to me, he spoke. "Don't worry, I myself will take you to the classes and introduce you to the students." He asserted.

Our conversation got interrupted when a Guard came running. He was gasping for breath, and wanted to say something.

"A labourer has fallen from the roof of the building under construction. He is in a critical state and very short of breath." He recited the whole story in one breath.

He spoke with such an apprehension of fear that compelled the attention of the whole gathering.

The Principal was transfixed. He went pale and felt uncomfortable. The drastic change of his facial expressions gave me a way to feel that there was something wrong and mysterious.... A slight feeling of suspicion crept over me.

"Sorry Tanmay, I'll have to leave." He set out the reasons hiding the expressions of anxiety. He ordered the guard to send Ambulance and walked away to avoid arousing suspicion.

In a hurry I had a look at my class schedule. All at once, I noticed a nasty murmuring close by. When I saw, it was the Hillbilly, who had carried my luggage to my room. I went close to him and tried to listen to his vague words.

"*It had to happen. What's strange about it? It had to happen. The doom's day is approaching; the destruction is at hand; no one will escape; everyone has to pay for it.... Oh God, what will happen? What will happen? What will happen now?*" he went repeating his words.

A gust of wind ruffled my thick brown hair. I was shocked to hear the Prophet of doom and a wave of dread swept over me. I felt a heavy feeling in the pit of my stomach and a sneaking suspicion though I was unaware of truth. His horrible facial expressions and vague words warned all doom and gloom. My mind got blocked and lost reasoning power. I felt pale, so pale that I nearly seemed to fade away in the bright morning sunshine. Meanwhile I felt a touch on my shoulder. With a jerk, I turned. It was Abhi.

"Dear, we are getting late for our classes." He reminded me.

I was stunned so I nodded only.

"Are you all right, dear? He asked.

"Ye ... Yeah... I'm all right." I said hesitatingly.

Indicating the Hillbilly "Don't take his words to your heart. He is a total nut case. He keeps talking to himself all the time." he gave a careless shrug and smile altogether.

My fright was turning to anger. "What a stupid fellow he is!..." going towards the Academic Building I muttered nervously and slapped my forehead.

Though Abhi's words had comforted me, the nasty words kept popping in and out of my mind. I couldn't shake the premonition, the heavy feeling of dread throughout the day.

CHAPTER THREE

The Exotic Blooms of the Orchid

It being my first teaching experience, I was quite excited and a bit nervous. I finally screwed up my courage and moved to the class room. We entered through the Reception, the most beautiful place in the entire campus. The rich curtains, cozy sofas, a charming table, attractive receptions counter gave the look of a well decorated interior of TV serials. There was a tall, slim and attractive lady attendant having melodious voice. She was wearing bright colored sari of the latest trend.

"Good morning sir! The lady wished gently. "Good morning!" regaining consciousness, I replied.

Reaching the counter, I handed her my appointment letter. She gave a cursory glance; opened a register, entered my name and placed it on the counter.

"Here is your name sir." The lady said gently.

I turned it to my side; put my signature and thanked the lady.

"Excuse me, Sir; you have class in 9th A and it's there in the Corridor." Pointing to the gate she said.

"Thank you very much." turning to the corridor, I replied.

Two-storied school building comprised of stylish classrooms, library, state of the art laboratories, high-tech computer lab, music and dance room and fully equipped communication infrastructure. Color, space and light combine to enhance the rooms, the corridors and the labs.

Abhi also had the class there so he led me to the Corridor. We stopped at the gate where the board read 9th A.

"This is your class sir." He informed.

"And one thing more Sir, be strict otherwise they won't listen you." He smiled a small smile.

"Bye. Sir.... ALL THE BEST" waving his hand, he said and disappeared from the scene.

Every aspect of teaching and learning here was supported by modern and relevant technology. Besides being equipped with Educomp, the classroom was well furnished with pleasing colors on the walls. To my right there was a very large black board covering almost half of the wall; to the left the future of our country was sitting all muddled up.

I stepped in complete disorder and found myself among a roaring crowd. All were busy merry making, chatting, gossiping, pulling and pushing each other. I was vaguely familiar with such an environment in the class.

A tall student who was strolling beside Podium glanced me, shouted at the top of his voice, **"*Kameeno chup ho jao.* Our new teacher has come."** His shouting gave way to hustle and bustle. The jostling, rushing were becoming all too familiar by degrees.

Those who listened stood up in honor; others were still unmindful to what's happening in the class. They were a sorry sight when they eventually sensed my presence.

However, the standup comedy lasted very soon with a warm wish.

"Goood Mo-r-ning Sir!" They grinned a serious welcome.

With that wish vanished the mischievous elf from the room and the faces resumed their innocence. One of them said, "He is our new English teacher from Bareilly, has come from B.H.U. (Kashi) to teach and preach both."

"Ha... Ha... Ha... Ha..." They grinned with delight.

I experienced a moment of panic as I vibrated my lips. Hardly had I opened my mouth when a thud sound echoed the room. The whole class again burst into laughter.

A student got up shamefacedly cleaning his hips. I thought about things in a careful and sensible way that I heard a faint murmur.

"What happened?" I asked the boy.

"Sorry sir, actually my seat is there in the corner" indicating an empty seat the boy said, "when you entered the class, I was chatting with my friends and couldn't manage to reach my seat in such a short time so I sat here. The seat was too small for three so I was pushed out."

The room was enlivened again with the echo of laughter. I had no option but to familiarize myself with the exotic blooms of the orchid. Emboldened by the excited rushing blood, I went over to introduce myself.

"Good morning! I'm Tanmay, your new English Teacher. I'm Post-Graduate from English Department, Banaras Hindu University." Catching a moment of silence in the class, I began, "Dear students! this is my first day and I hope it is a pleasantly cool room.... You all are looking sweet, gentle, and I expect an affectionate, civilized and, gentle demeanor from you all. So be quite attentive and sincere to my teachings in the class." I addressed them with an easy familiarity that made them feel at home.

After exchanging the usual pleasantries, we got down to serious discussion.

"Education is the greatest asset that you can possess. Good education prepares one to become a capable, competent and responsible member of the society. Character building and inculcation of the moral values is an essential part of a good education system, but it is possible only with your genial cooperation. The fun and frolic is undoubtedly important at your age, but sincerity is all the more essential."

I saw a flicker of smile on a few figures.

"Don't laugh, it's a serious suggestion." I added.

My words created a magic on their minds and abruptly they became serious, and started listening me. I was happy to see the positive response of my teaching that was preaching from their point of view.

I decided to interact with the students so that I may be familiar with the young motivated individuals. I made a few figures stand and introduce themselves.

A tall boy, thin and lanky with scraggly blonde hair stood up first.

"My name is Vikas means 'development'. But since I am born, there is no development in my parents' life. Consequently they have sent me here for my development."

"Ha... Ha... Ha... Ha." whoops of delight echoed the room.

"You" indicating another student, I said.

She was a short, stubby girl of tough-looking, with spiky black hair.

"My name is Rakhi. My father was a great fan of the Bollywood star RAKHI."

"Who—Rakhi Sawant?" a boy interrupted.

"Ha... Ha... Ha... Ha." The whole class whooped it up.

"Shut up. I won't stand for any nonsense." The girl got angry, but after a pause she resumed.

"My parents are doctors in govt. Hospital. They want me to be a Doctor also. So for better education and environment they have dumped me here." Saying this, she sat down.

"My name is Badal." Next student having a big fat belly overhung his belt introduced. Since I was born on a stormy day when 'clouds' were rumbling.... My parents are big corporate. They had no time for me so they sent me here." he said grimly.

"Hello sir, I am Saurabh," a cute face who was busy nudging his friends, stood up, "I was a great fan of Sachin Tendulkar so I loved playing cricket all the time. On the other hand, my father who's a Professor wanted to see books in my hands rather than cricket bat. He advised me a lot, but I didn't listen. Consequently, he got angry and sent me here." He was depressed when he sat down.

"Sir, My name is Prakash," next student got up brusquely, "my father is an M.P. All the mafias of the division are after him. He sent me here because of the fear of being kidnapped." He said with flush of anger in his eyes; paused, raised his head again and burst; "Now I am kidnapped here. My parents come and pay the ransom to let me remain kidnapped."

No one laughed in the class now. The blooming faces turned into grave, solemn and earnest statues. When enlivened, their eyes were misted with tears. Some were using hankies to clean their blurred vision.

Each face in the class had a story behind his tears. They were the most shining stars of the galaxy of their respective families, but now they were estranged by those who loved them most. At such a painful turn of situation, I tried to soothe the students' heart:

"Dear students! Our parents don't have any grudges against us. They send us to schools so that we can learn together and develop wider horizons than our family can provide. The atmosphere set by a boarding school is best suited for learning and recreation. It is a family that enables us to inculcate a healthy culture. Your parents have deserted you at the tender age because they wanted to provide a healthy educational base and lay the strongest foundation for the successful future of their lovely kids. The boarding school imbibes a sense of discipline in children. Here you are taught to follow a schedule and strictly obey the rules formulated. Good habits, such as sleeping on time, waking up early and exercising, get developed automatically, once you become a part of a residential school. Here you are responsible for yourself and have no protective shield over you. Consequently, you are independent, bold and fearless, ready to face any undesirable situation alone. I was also estranged when I was younger than you even." Seeing everyone mesmerized, I took a pause.

"We are a family here," I resumed. "Now we'll share every fun, joy, sorrow and never let anyone feel lonely.... Are you ready to be the truest part of it?" I asked.

Next moment, I heard a big uproar in my favor, "yes sir." The faces that had lost their luster, resumed the glow.

"Well, I'm sorry you've lost your shoes, but you've got to laugh, haven't you?" I joked apart.

This times the laughter was not that much coarse. It had a pleasant note to the ear. We had formed a new galaxy here with these new shining stars moving around and gaining knowledge all the time.

The bell having rung, I stepped out of the class. It was painful to be alone again. That single day had brought to my notice many sides of the personality of the boarders. On the one hand, they were naughty beyond the proper limit whereas on the other, they had a heart too full of the milk of human kindness and affection.

Out of the academic building, Abhi had been talking to the teachers beside the fountain.

"Tanmay" raising his hand he shouted loudly.

I went to him. He introduced me to the teachers there. They invited me to have lunch together that I accepted pronto. Sharing a few moments of get together over lunch table, we retired to our rooms for siesta.

CHAPTER FOUR

A Gasp of Horror

I slept solidly. The warmth of my quilt against chill abroad kept me asleep and I went through the morning and the rest of the day with all the things I pictured going through my mind and when they came together in one final, horrible ending, I twisted and turned in bed. The sun had lowered behind the trees. It was nearly five in the evening when the Intercom bell tolled me back from the sound sleep. I blinked several times, trying to clear my mind. My neck felt stiff and the back ached. I raised my hand to the receiver.

"Hello Tanmay, Good evening! This is principal speaking." I heard a voice. The words 'pri-n-ci-pal' echoed, and in a moment the drowsiness ran away. I rubbed the sleep from my eyes.

"Good evening, Sir!" I responded.

"Tanmay, there is a meeting at 6 pm in my office. Reach here in time." He informed.

"OK sir, I'll be there in time." Yawning I said.

"Have you taken your refreshment?" He inquired.

"Not yet. I have just woken up with your call, sir." I replied.

"OK. Get up easily. Take your refreshment and be here at 6." With these words he put the receiver.

I climbed to my feet and stretched my árms above my head, trying to stretch away my stiff neck. I felt a cold chill down my back so wrapped myself well in woolen clothes before leaving for Cafeteria. The silence in hostel notified that the Imps had already left.

"Good evening! Tanmay" I heard a familiar voice on my way to Cafeteria.

It was Abhi with his never failing stick in his hands.

"Good evening, Abhi." I replied with equal warmth.

"Do you know about the meeting at 6?" Drawing my attention, he asked.

"Yeah, Principal Sir gave me a call and informed?" I answered.

"Really, Froggy gave you a call. Amazing!" He cast the humor of his own brand.

"Gosh, who's this Froggy? I didn't get you." I expressed my surprise.

"Who else? Of course, our principal. It's his sobriquet. Don't you know?" We both laughed our heads off when he spoke with his unfailing good humor.

"By the way, have you taken Refreshment?" he asked inquisitively.

"Just going." I replied.

"Let's have together." Pulling my hand he ushered me in Cafeteria.

The students had taken their refreshment and were moving for Prep Classes in line. The scene was of a healthy discipline. I was glad to see the students instructed, administered and schooled in habits which tend them toward the formation of good character. The school constituted a little world in itself, and in it the students had to encounter many of the trials that beset everyone in life.

The sun had set much before and the fog had started spreading its wings. We couldn't withstand the chilling wind outside so we took shelter in Froggy's office. A few teachers were already there.

Froggy entered a few minutes later and presided over the meeting. Some important issues regarding Half Yearly Exams, hygiene and discipline of the students in hostels were discussed.

"Tanmay, you are now a member of our family. Enjoy the boarding life and get used to it; then we'll assign some duties to you." Froggy said placing his left hand around my shoulder. The meeting dispersed soon.

I along with Abhi came out and refreshed ourselves looking at the rising fountain in the open. Though it was extreme chilled, I couldn't stop myself playing with the tiny drops of water splashing all around.

At a distance, I noticed the appearance of the sizzling beauty. The blooming Princess of the last night caught my eye once more. I turned to her. She was tall, slender, too young and good-looking; not an ounce of fat but still shapely, with a good high bustline. She wasn't wearing makeup. She had naturally full sable brows and lashes. Her heavy dark black hair was bound up in a horsetail to keep it off her shoulders and the back of her neck. Her coloring was sallow, as if she stayed indoors the year around. She was looking fabulous in her heavy red-and-white plaid sky sweater. She wore black leggings that made her look even taller.

Her hands glittered like stars and sweet voice fell like a gentle fragrance. Her face was more endearing than God and there was innocence in her manner.

When we exchanged glances, I felt that agreeable little buzz in my heart. Suddenly the funny event—the boy running with her stall flashed back—and I smiled a small smile. She also gave me a smile of acknowledgement. She had a dimple in both the cheeks when she smiled.

"Hello Tanmay, how are you?" I received a high five disturbing the heavenly view.

When I spun around, I noticed a young man in his thirties, well-built in structure and almost 6 ft height. He was the same man who was sitting in front of me in the meeting. Before I could come out of the rapture of the beautiful sight and utter anything, I heard a faint murmur.

"I am Rishabh, the warden of senior boys." He introduced himself while shaking hands.

"Nice to meet you!" While shaking hands I admitted.

"By the way, you enjoy the beautiful evening. I'm going to hostel for a long soak in a hot bath." He smiled with relief.

"I would like to join you. I have to arrange my things in my room."

"Then come. Let's go" he suggested.

We started moving to our respective rooms discussing the school and hostel life. On the way he informed me that the school provided good and proper facilities for the keepsake of the health of students. There was a well equipped medical room. Very skilled professionals were in attendance all the time to ensure all emergencies. The medical room provided complete first aid facilities, all important medicines, proper diagnosis and management referred services to specified center as per consent of the ward's parents. The regular checkups were also done by specialists; the proper medical records were maintained and valuable suggestions were provided to students for being fit, physically as well as mentally and emotionally.

Reaching my room, I arranged my entire luggage at proper places so that I could get them easily whenever I needed. The flower I got in the morning was quite beautiful and lovely. I placed that in a flower pot on the table and sat down to read my books.

All of a sudden, the corridor got enlivened with loud noises and a great hustle-bustle. In a flash I became aware that the students were returning after taking dinner. When the students settled in the hostel, and there was less noise coming from the corridor, I got up, gave a call and asked the Head Cook to send my dinner in my room.

I resumed my study again. A little while later, I heard the same sweet voice,

"Sir Ji, Open the door. Your dinner is ready." The small boy said.

I opened the gate; he entered; placed the tray on the table and went to fill my jug.

"Lovely boy" I said to myself.

"Sir Ji, do you need anything else or I should leave?" The boy asked again on returning.

"Wait a second" coming out with towel in my hands I said. I took a ten rupee note out of my shirt's pocket.

"Take a chocolate from the canteen tomorrow." I said handing him the note with affection.

"Thank you sir" he ran away singing and crooning.

I sat down to have my dinner. In the interim I heard some funny noises coming and someone scolding the students. I guessed Rishabh would be on duty.

"You enemies of my last birth! Go to your beds fast." he was growling.

"Hey you wicked fellow! Where is your night suit?"

"Sir, I have given that for washing. It has gone for iron now." The students were coming up with excuses.

"All the students must be in their beds by the count of 10." Then the countdown started ... 10... 9...8...7...6 and so on.

The same activities were going on in the other room also. There Abhi was tackling the junior Imps, but he was a bit more aggressive. He was giving the students nicely so the students were listening at the speed of lightening. A few students were sobbing and complaining.

The school dormitory had a 'lights out' time at 10 p.m. when the students were required to be in bed, and no talking was permitted after that. Such rules were difficult to enforce, and the Imps often tried to break them—by reading surreptitiously by torchlight or escaping on nocturnal excursions. As a routine, the lights in the dormitory were off.

I was feeling entertained by the way things were happening in the hostel. But I concentrated to my book again.

"Who's there celebrating his honeymoon?" Rishabh asked switching on the light in the hostel a few minutes later. "You can't sleep without your wife?" Rishabh asked humiliating a student.

The entire hostel echoed with the laughter. I also sat straight being amused at the remark of the Warden.

Actually, each student had got a bed to sleep in still they used to sleep together. Rishabh had come to check whether they were sleeping in their respective beds.

The scenes of high spirit and jollity made me bounce from my seat so I came out of my room and started strolling in the corridor.

Rishabh switched off the light in the senior dormitory again. When he saw me looking at the twinkling stars in the sky, he came to me.

"Hello dear, enjoying the beauty of the stars?" he asked me.

"Yeah, it's really beautiful to enjoy the scenic beauty of the shining stars here among the hills at night. It soothes my heart and shares the loneliness." I exclaimed with joy.

"By the way, you are quite sarcastic and funny in your remarks." I said giving a smile.

"I have to be. Actually, they are so shameless that whatever you say falls flat on them. For a few seconds, they'll listen and the moment you get loose, they are the same old naughty ones." He said getting irritated.

"It's pretty late now. So, go and take rest." I suggested.

"What about you? Don't you feel like sleeping" he asked before taking a turn.

"I have to write a Research Paper for an International Seminar in B.H.U. so I'll wake up till late night." I replied softly.

"OK, Good night" he retired to sleep.

"Good night" I exchanged words.

Again the deep limitless firmament full of luminaries was before my eyes. When I looked down, there was a vast spread thick garden. The pale light from the crescent moon trickled onto the glistening, wet grass. I felt very unusual seeing the Hillbilly entering the garden such late night hours and going towards the Building under construction.

Forgetting all this I returned to my studies and gave full concentration to write the Research Paper. Sitting on my bed, I meditated for a few minutes and restored my concentration. It took me almost two hours to write the first draft of my Research Paper. I took a sigh of relief and planned to take a round in the corridor to enjoy the fresh cool air. It was very cold outside and a chill wind was blowing. I couldn't stand the ice freezing temperature so I decided to return my room and enjoy the warmth of quilt. I was to turn that I again saw the Hillbilly coming out of the garden.

"It's extremely cold out there even then he is walking abroad at midnight. Is he a man or spirit?" I shuddered at the thought and a wave of cold fear swept over me.

I kept watching him for a few seconds and saw him going to the side where the fourth grade employees were given accommodation. He entered a room; closed the door and switched off the light a little while later.

Hillbilly's activities caused many a question race through my mind. I shivered with fear as I answered my own questions.

"I know why he doesn't feel the extreme chill out there", I thought backing away from the Corridor.

"I know he is not a man of flesh and blood". Trembling all over, I wrapped my arms around my chest, as if shielding myself from my frightening thoughts.

Overcoming with fear, I uttered a low moan and backed away from the chill into the preferred safety of my room. My legs felt trembly and weak. I turned off the lights, and climbed into bed. Now I was in bed listening to the silence and trying to force away the frightening thoughts that crowded my mind. But I couldn't stop my mind from whirring over all that had happened. His gloomy words 'Doom's day is at hand' were still dancing in my eyes. The bed took some time to get warm. Pretty soon, I was caressed by the sweet sleep.

CHAPTER FIVE

Suspense—What will Happen Next?

In the morning, I stirred a little, but I didn't wake. Pretty soon I reminded that I'm not at my home, but in boarding school. I jumped out of bed; switched on light; it was 7 am. I thumped my head with my right hand; twisted my face and prepared to go to bed again. It was really biting cold. Rubbing my hand, I slipped in bed and had hardly arranged my quilt when I sighted one more flower placed at the table. The sleep in my eyes ran away. Jumping up I reached to the table; picked up the flower. It was the same old flower. Then I searched for the last day's flower. It was in the vase where I left it. I was looking at both the flowers. They were identical in look. Confusion, bewilderment was at the extreme to know how it was possible that a flower reached my room daily without my noticing it. In excitement, I left the bed; wore my jacket; peeped out of the balcony.

It was a magnificent morning. The rain drops collected in pits declared a soft rain fall last night. The garden with green leaves, multi-colored flowers and dew drops on them made my heart feel "garden and garden". The sun had not risen yet. The clouds were travelling in the sky bearing gallons of water. Above all, it was heart capturing to be a part of this beautiful scene.

I pulled myself in the room; closed the biting cold outside and warmed myself wrapping in bed sheet. The thought of the flower's unnoticed reaching in my room was indigestible. To warm up mind and body, I gave order in Cafeteria to send me a cup of tea only. The prolonged discussion in mind couldn't find any solution to the problem.

"Sir, your tea." The small boy uttered softly entering my room.

I indicated to the table. He placed the cup there. I looked puzzled so he returned without speaking anything further.

Finding myself helpless, I concentrated to have sips of warm tea in chilled weather. The tea in cup was almost over, but mind hadn't started working.

Time has the solution of all the problems. Keeping it in mind, I dropped the flower issue and got ready for the school. Since, it was extremely cold, I wore warm clothes with black coat.

I didn't feel like taking breakfast so I decided to go to the classes directly. At 9:15 I left the room for the school. Near the garden, Froggy was standing, talking to an old lady. He called me:

"Tanmay, Good Morning!"

"Good Morning!" The sobriquet 'Froggy' I muttered silently.

What happened? Not looking cheerful; anything serious?" He asked.

"Nothing as such. Actually I am not used to such chilled weather so I am a bit perturbed."

"By the way, how was your experience of the classes yesterday?

"It was a pleasant experience. The students are full of the joys of spring, but pretty co-operative. We need to tickle their sensibilities. But anyhow I'll manage with them easily." I assured him.

"Exactly, you have felt their pulse in a jiffy. I'm confident of your abilities now." he uttered in appreciation.

"Oh, by the way, Tanmay" indicating the old lady he said, "meet, she is Vidhya, the warden of senior Girls' Hostel."

"Hello ma'am!"

"Hello sir!"

There was nothing feminine in her hound-heavy face; only the amazing cliff of her bosom served as a landmark of her sex. She was quite old at the age of retirement. Her face and skin on hands were wrinkled yet she covered her old age marks on face well. But she seemed to have a close affinity and rapport with Froggy.

"Have a nice day!" I wished both of them and went on my way.

When I reached my classroom, the students were anxiously waiting for me. They all were looking decent and civilized unlike the previous day.

"Sir, today we want to watch *Romeo Juliet* on Educomp if you allow" all spoke in one voice. "It's not a part of our syllabus still we hope for a favorable reply from you. Tomorrow onwards, we'll follow every instruction of yours considering God's will."

"It took me a few moments to decide in their favor.

"Who's the Prefect of the class?" I asked.

"A handsome and tall student stood up. He was the same student who reported the case in Dining Hall and the yesterday's downfall in class.

"What's your name?

"Sir, my name is Vaibhav." He answered in a humble way.

"Can you please come forward and help me?

He came to me; started dragging the board to the right. Hidden behind the large board, there was a very big screen. A few more boys came to our help. They switched on CPU and logged on computer. Through Educomp, they started the animation movie. They all enjoyed it, but every time they seemed restless waiting for the *kissing scene*. When the long awaited moment arrived, they were dumb silent; stopped taking breaths; didn't wink at all.

The bell having rung, they turned off the system, shifted the board at its proper place.

"Thank you sir, you are great. We are big fan of yours."

I came out of the class. A few cute girls came out rushing behind me.

"Thank you, sir. You are so nice." They spoke together.

"Well, how do the students feel when I'm in the class?" I asked them affectionately.

"Sir, the students here are academically inclined children. They are self motivated. They don't want to be over-pressurized or compelled for study. If a teacher allows them a little freedom, they are ready to follow his every instruction without delay." One of them replied.

The clock had already struck 2 when I reached Dining Hall and enjoyed a variety of dishes served in lunch. Ad interim, I heard some strange voices mixed with weeping outside. I finished my lunch hurriedly and envisaged a great hubbub.

The guards at the gate were not allowing the people to enter so they were shouting from the gate and calling the Principal.

I stepped to the gate to look into the matter.

Before anyone could speak, the guard, who received me at Gate No. 1, came rushing to me.

"Sir, don't go near them. They are the co-workers of the man who fell from the Building under construction yesterday."

"What happened? Is there anything serious?" I felt the things were looking grim.

"Sir, actually the laborer has collapsed." He said grimly.

"Oh, my God!"

"Sir, you have seen that laborer." he spoke heightening my confrontation.

"I have seen!... When and where?" I asked astonishingly.

"He is the same laborer who denied carrying your luggage on the first day."

"Oh, that one!" I felt traumatized; a sense of gloom clouded my reasoning. I took a turn feeling deep in my heart; a pain for the untimely death of the laborer. I was on my way to hostel that I sighted Hillbilly again in the garden moving here and there restlessly and mumbling.

"*It had to happen. What's strange about it?" It had to happen. The destruction is at hand; the doom's day is approaching; no one will escape; everyone has to pay for it. Oh God! what will happen? What will happen? What will happen now?*"

His doomed words stabbed at me like knives. I felt myself at the Death's door.

CHAPTER SIX

Birthday Party

It being a monsoon evening, I sighted the best sunset of my life. The evening had spread its wings to envelop the day. I was sipping tea in my room. I had just got up from a sound sleep so feeling pretty relaxed. In the intervening time, a few students came to my room.

"Good evening sir! May we come in?" they asked reverently.

"Yeah, come in. Sit on the settee."

It was the senior most lot. Chirag, Mayank and Abhinav entered and sat. They were in Jeans and House T-shirts.

"How are you feeling here sir?" they asked humbly.

"Pretty cool! The school environment and you all…everything is fabulous."

"How is your study going on?"

"Well." They replied.

"Actually Sir, we are going to Cafeteria to take refreshment, and to celebrate the birthday of a small girl Deep Shikha, the student of class 5th. Sir, please join us there. We'll enjoy a lot. We like your company. …One thing more Sir; if you need any help, please give us a call anytime. We are ready even to die for your sake." Chirag said.

They all went to the Cafeteria with the Warden. In a flash, I also got up; the blue Coat was on and looking amazingly handsome. On reaching Cafeteria, I saw the students enjoying snacks and milk.

"Hello Tanmay!" Abhi and Rishabh were waiting for me.

"Good evening!"

"Good evening!"

"Hey Chhotu, bring refreshment for us."

"Sir, kindly have a seat." Abhi requested.

I had hardly finished my Refreshment that I was surrounded by a bevy of beauties.

"Good evening sir!"

"Good evening!" I was taken away from the Wardens forcibly.

Seeing the girls, some frolicsome boys also came.

"Hello sir, May we join the beautiful company?"

"Yeah, sure. Come."

"Sir, you have got a very pleasing demeanor. Whenever we are with you, we feel that we are with our friends."

"By the way sir, if you don't mind, can we ask something, something personal.... Bareilly is above 750 KM away from here. Why did you think of coming so far?" Chirag asked inquisitively.

"Yeah, it's really personal. You are right. I think there might be a relation of the previous birth!" The students gave a genial smile at my funny answer.

"I had hardly spoken the words that a big black feline jumped from nowhere upon the glasses placed on the table and broke them by making them fall on floor.

The noise was so nasty and cacophonous that we had to close our ears. The life stooped for a few seconds with the disturbance and amazement of all.

In a couple of seconds, everyone was back to his work and the small boy in the Cafeteria was collecting the broken pieces of glasses.

The girls came close to me. "Sir, please do us a favor."

"What kind of favor?"

"Ask the Wardens to let us dance during Birthday celebration. Please sir, only you can do so. They are so pally with you that they will readily accept.... Do it sir, please...we'll never forget your kind favor."

I was engrossed what to do that a very sweet little girl came to me.

"Good evening sir, please listen to me."

She was so cute with her big brown eyes and curly black hair down to her shoulders that the world around seemed so drab and colorless next to her. My soft heart was so touched by the softness in her voice that I instantly sat on my knees.

"Yes, my sweet darling! Why do you scatter the pearls of your words?"

"Sir, it's my birthday today. We are going to celebrate. Don't go anywhere. This is my humble request." She chirped happily.

I was so emotional hearing her words that I embraced her tightly; kissed her on both the cheeks.

"Happy birthday dear!" Looking straight into her eyes, I said.

"May I know the name of my little Angel?"

"Deep Shikha" she smiled and went to her Warden who had been looking at us.

"Sir, please talk to our Wardens." Chirag and his group forced again.

"OK. I'll do my best." I promised and went to the Wardens.

"Tanmay, have you learnt some magic? These students are a big nuisance; they never listen to anyone but to the contrary they are running after you." Rishabh passed a cheery remark.

"Tomorrow onwards they won't run after." I murmured faintly.

"Is there anything serious?" Rishabh asked holding my hand.

"Actually they are demanding a thing that is not in my hands."

"What's that?

"Group Dance" I said very softly.

Rishabh thought for a few seconds and spoke, "Don't worry, I'll manage."

Now the celebration started; an enormously big cake was laid on the table. The students surrounded from all sides. Cafeteria was totally packed. The inflated balloons were in the hands of students ready to be burst. The candles were lighted; the sweet little Angel was given a new knife. She looked at every one; gave a long smile and raised her hand to cut the Cake.

The first piece of Cake she offered to her Warden who was standing nearby. The Warden bent down; turned her hand; inserted the piece in her mouth and the remaining she ate herself. There was a merry din of clapping and bursting of balloons. All were rejoicing and nearing close to the birthday girl.

"Music on" Rishabh came to the front and woofers in Cafeteria became alive. He started dancing with his wife Radhika. The music set everyone's feet tapping. The students formed a circle around Rishabh and started dancing. Over all, the scene was so pleasing that all the teachers had to share in dance.

Rishabh came to me smiling and hugged me.

"Thank you, sir." I paid my reverence.

"All right! Anything for you!"

A little while later, the birthday girl was moving all around with the Waiter requesting the teachers to taste Cake.

"God bless you my sweet little angel." I said taking a piece of Cake.

Chirag and his group came rushing and made me dance with them. When the song was over, they dragged me to have a walk in the lush green garden. We were out sitting on the green grass talking to each other. The faces of the students reflected the amount of happiness they were feeling.

All of a sudden I sighted Hillbilly again in the Garden.

"Who's that old man, Chirag?

"Who—that old man?" he raised his finger.

"Yeah—that old fellow!" I agreed.

"Sir, he's Gardner in our school." Looking at the old man, he said.

"Actually Chirag, at times he behaves like a cynic."

"Sir, he is not normal so he keeps on whispering all the time."

"But his language is very ominous."

"Sir, he is like this only; a gone case; don't take him seriously."

I breathed more freely as this harmless interpretation of the words of Doom-Merchant forced itself upon me. I heaved a sigh of relief; spread my legs to the front and hands to back for support. The old man who looked horrendous was busy in his affair. I felt I was distressing myself uselessly.

"Good evening, Ma'am!" Chirag wished someone.

My train of thoughts stopped all of a sudden. I looked at the side where Chirag was looking and saw a beautiful face getting closer. I was pretty confirmed that she was the same lady whom I saw the first night with a stick in her hands.

"Hello Tanmay! How are you?"

"I'm just fine!" I replied amiably.

"I was hunting for you everywhere." She said.

The image of the child being beaten flashed back all of a sudden. But I was dead sure that I had not committed any mistake so there was no question of being beaten.

One more thought ran across my mind lest the students had committed any mistake in my name like—"They had placed a flower in her room daily or worse than that—they might have dropped a letter— love letter—and convinced her that it's me who was doing this."

'If any of these is true, the consequences can be serious.' I felt puzzled and bamboozled. But I dared to ask hesitatingly.

"Why? Is there anything serious?" I asked with a blank gaze.

"No! Nothing serious!"

"By the way, (raising her hand) I am Aanya."

The next moment her hand was in my hand.

"Nice to meet you!" I said shaking hand.

Seeing us sitting together, Chirag went away stealthily waving his hand to say 'bye'.

"Actually the preparations for Teacher's Day have started. Each and every teacher has to perform on stage. My name is there with you for duet song or group dance." She informed.

"You can't be serious!"

She nodded and confirmed the gravity of the decision.

"Is it mandatory to perform?" I asked anxiously.

"Yeah, they say so." She looked crestfallen.

"But I am good at neither. If I sang even by mistake, they'll put fingers in their ears." I admitted plainly.

"The same here! But I have learnt dancing during my schooling. If you are ready, I can make you learn a few steps." She spoke with a smile.

"I'm ready to handover myself if you can make one learn dance in a couple of days." I stated.

"It's not a competition, and we are not professional dancers. We just have to do it for the sake of students." She justified.

"When are we going to have a rehearsal?" I asked excitedly.

"We'll do it tomorrow onwards in the evening if you are free." She suggested.

"Yeah, sure I am ready." I answered without delay.

"Will you stay here or move to hostel?" she asked softly.

"It's getting pretty dark here. I'll move to my room." I opened my mouth.

"Then come. Let's go together. What are you waiting for?" She said giving her hand to me in support.

I took her hand again in my hand. Earlier her fingers were in my hand now wrist. The softness of her hand that I failed to feel first time was pleasing my heart.

"Thank you" I let her hand go; cleaned my jeans at hips and started pacing with the Beauty personified.

She was quite professional so she discussed everything but personal lives. All over the time, the students, their lives were the burning issues. Reaching our floor, she moved to right and I to left. Our rooms were adjacent but the stairs in between. I had turned the key in lock; opened the lock and door, but I wanted to see her going in room so I was standing holding the handle in my hands.

She took some time, but when she entered, she had a look at me and said, "Bye."

Perhaps this was the word, I was waiting for. I enclosed myself once more in the four walls.

CHAPTER SEVEN

A Kafkaesque Nightmare

The mystery prevailing had made me a night-owl. It was a Guy Fawkes Night so I returned late into my room after having dinner. I was quite exhausted and it was just not physically possible to finish all my pending work by the end of the week.

"I'll wear myself out if I carry on waking up late nights and working so hard." I pondered over the ponderous point.

Tiredness had easily crept up on me while arranging my luggage all day long. Hence I dropped the idea of struggling with the books. I took out my night suit from the cupboard and changed.

I opened the window to let the fresh air rush in. The messengers of rain were playing hide and seek with the Moon abroad and the fast pacing winds warned a heavy rain fall.

The chill in the air compelled me to wrap myself in the heavy quilt. The rising warmth inside sent a sound sleep soon to my exhausted mind.

A sinewy black Shadow followed me into my room. It set a trap for me and I walked straight into it. I was trapped in wreck. The place was isolated and one of the remotest areas of the world. I reached the accursed place following the shadow, blasphemous abnormality from Hell's nethermost craters; a nameless, unstructured abomination which no mind could fully grasp and no pen even partly describe.

I was moving in unknown land for some unknown reason. I had no idea where I was going. I was headed deeper and deeper in the woods, a deep black hole that didn't seem to end. The scenes had morbid look. There was thunder in the air at night. The fear was lurking from all the corners of spectral and desolate ruins. The figure at stone walls looked grotesque and terrible. Everything was strange and full of horror. The ghastly noises were deafening my ears. The whole landscape was surrounded in the lake of darkness.

The trees were unnaturally large and twisted. The creepers climbing the trees reminded me of the dangerous snakes. The stones with bizarre shapes looked like dead men's skulls.

The uneven earth was covered with the blood and human debris. The large amount of bones scattered bespoke too vividly the ravages of the demon teeth and talons. The poor creatures had been destroyed in such a cruel manner, that their carcasses were horribly mangled and were giving a horrid smell. The annals of debris manifested carnage. It had been a sinister mansion among high hills.

The shadow was dancing before my eyes and changing shapes at every stage. I was hypnotized so helpless to return. I was taken to blind cave; given scary offerings; tickled by skeletons hanging from trees. The shadow disappeared leaving me all alone among ruins. The flying skulls blocked my way. I was shivering and gibbering. I tried to run harder, but I wasn't going anywhere. I was confused, tortured, tormented and oppressed by the agents of the Shadow.

I felt let down against the lethal attack of misfortunes. I sat down and began to shed tears. The storms of sobbing and the rumbling of bitter weep were so horrendous that it shook me all over with an unknown awed silence. In that shrieking, the inmost soul of human fear and agony clawed hopelessly and insanely at the ebony gates of oblivion. I awoke to red madness and the mockery of diabolism, as farther and farther down inconceivable vistas that phobic and crystalline anguish retreated and reverberated.

The approaching thunder and lightning brought me back from the land of dead to the world of living. I woke up with a loud cry. I sat up dizzily and rubbed my eyes. The nightmare of creeping death made my hair stand on its end. In my sleep I had just seen apocalyptic visions. I collected myself and wiped the drops of sweat resulting from nightmare. Images of the horrifying dream floated back to me.

I was sitting in my bed all covered and wiping the drops of sweat from my face. The bedclothes were also damp from perspiration. The air in the room hung heavy and bitter. I kicked off the quilt and lowered my feet to the floor. I felt shaky when I clicked on the light. I made my way to the cupboard, took a clean nightshirt and changed.

The restlessness in bed led me to the Corridor where I saw the reflection of my tribulation. The clouds were rumbling; the lightning was cleaving the chest of the sky. The rain was pouring in buckets outside. Extremely chilled wind was howling and thumping my body. The fear of landslide and landslip was all the more chilling.

Though I was in bed now shutting the entire chill outside, but the heart was still restless behind the ribs. Long brooding was driving me maniac. Never before had the presence of evil so poignantly oppressed me. Later I must have dropped asleep again, for it was out of a phantasmal chaos that my mind leaped when the night grew hideous with shrieks beyond anything in my former experience or imagination.

CHAPTER EIGHT

Rose: An Unsolved Mystery

The dream at night was so full of horror that it had survived the trauma of waking. I opened my eyes to come out of the world of fantasy, so got up in bed. The eyes were still close and the body covered in quilt from top to bottom. I opened my eyes very slowly to see the light of the day as if the eyes had been operated, and the doctor had suggested parting the lids cautiously.

The eyes were all right. The light of the day was visible. I dared to come out of warm bed to the chill of morning. When I went to the window, the snow down the hill sparkled brightly. For a brief second, I saw a reindeer trotting into a thick cluster of pines.

I stretched, smiling as the fresh morning air floated in through my open window. But my congenial mood vanished as soon as the awful memory of the night before swept back into my mind.

I was befuddled by the horror of the day—a fresh rose on the table. I closed my eyes and ran madly to bed turning back. I breathed in or out only when I covered myself well from top to bottom. The chilling in body from any corner was making me feel the presence of someone in my room. The panic had done all the damage. The heart had resumed its fast face behind the ribs like last night. The only difference was that I shrieked loudly at night, but now the voice in throat had died away.

I was stumped for solution of the bizarre and weird happenings with me. Lying in bed, I summoned the session of rational thoughts and analyzed the sinister occurrences. The result was even more frightening. An idea struck my mind lest the room be haunted.

Placing my right hand on left side of chest, I consoled the fast beating heart with magic words "All is well. All is well." But to get the result faster, I placed both the hands on the heart and realized, "Nothing is well. Nothing is well."

Ultimately, the heart relaxed; the confidence restored. I put the quilt aside and got out of bed. The eyes still rested on the flower. I reluctantly went to the table with the pace of a snail, touched the flower with thousands of currents running in mind and finally picked it up with a jolt. The heart also felt a jolt of dismay. I made a minute survey of my room all around and found the balcony gate unbolted. I retreated to my bed; rested myself comfortably and tried to efface the horror from mind.

I had to engage the classes so I got ready and set out to see the blooming flowers in the classes. The entire school was covered with the dense clouds of fog and mist. I could hardly see at a distance.

"Good Morning, Sir." I heard a sweet child like voice. I recognized easily that it was the little Birthday girl well covered in thick woolen clothes. She was playing in the Park. Seeing me passing from there, she came rushing to me.

"Good Morning! My dear angel," I said looking at her out of utmost affection.

I held her in my arms and pressed close to my heart. Her face, activities, warmth, love and affection brought her so close to me that I was extra conscious for her. I had established a close affinity and rapport with the Sweet Bud.

"How are you? How is your study going on?" I fondled.

"I am fine and my study is also satisfactory." She said with a style.

"OK, my love, now you go and play. I'm going to see how the preparation for the Teacher's Day is going on?" I said indicating to the Park.

"OK Sir, Bye. Have a nice day!" she said going to the Park side.

I was on my way again. Near the fountain, I heard a female choir "Good Morning Sir".

I turned to the side of wish and sighted Aanya counseling a few girls. I reached her and stood silently.

"Tanmay, please don't go anywhere. The preparation is in full swing so the classes will not run today. We also have to rehearse." She spoke enthusiastically. "These girls along with boys will dance with us and we have to play a lead role. We are going to the Common Hall for Dance practice. Please join us there."

She kept on speaking without looking into my eyes whereas I was reading the redness of her face because of chilled weather and sighting the steam coming out of her mouth with every word she spoke.

"Yeah, I'm ready, but allow me to change these formals. I'll feel a little bit uncomfortable while dancing in this attire." I uttered showing my helplessness.

"Sure, you go and change your clothes. We'll meet there in 15 minutes. I have sent for boys. They are also coming." She spoke softly.

"Bye." She said looking into my eyes.

Soon I lost sight of her and myself in the clouds of fog.

A few minutes later, I was in the auditorium with doors all shut and a high pitch music on.

The couples were standing side-by-side in two facing lines with all the boys on one side and girls on the other. The dancing pairs were not fixed. The boys progressed down the line moving in walking or skipping steps in symmetrical figures. They moved in a way so that they might change partners, thus they danced at least a little with every member of the opposite sex.

Since I was not open to such stage performances so a bit hesitation was blocking my steps.

"Hello Tanmay! You come here close to me. Hold me like this; place your hand on my waist; bear my weight when I whirl around you." She instructed me along with the other pairs.

There was such electricity when I placed my hand on her waist for the first time. The warm steam from her mouth tickled my cheeks; the puffed up breasts raised restlessness. I was entrenched by the silken feel of her hair against my cheek and felt an electric charge from her lips brushing my ear. I was dancing with the globe of beauty in my hands, and feeling my heart pound and my hands sweat. My thudding heart and speeding pulse were revolting. When she held me and guided me around the dance floor, I felt different than with anyone else. None of my other dance partners affected me that way.

By the end of the dance lesson I knew that I wanted to see her again despite being the teacher in school. She felt the same way because as we walked out together she asked if I wanted to go for a cup of coffee. We talked until the Cafeteria got closed.

I think it was her eyes that convinced me enough to stay and we simply enjoyed each other's company until it got late and we had to retire our respective rooms. When I closed the door after she bade 'good bye', I knew that I didn't have to panic. I had found someone that understood who I was, no matter how strange or complicated I was. I knew that I had found someone that I could love without being afraid to love. From then on it was clear that there was something special between us.

The room was warm with the smell of roses. I was happy to be her friend. The train of thoughts was obstructed by the entry of a student.

"Good evening Sir! May I come in?" Chirag was standing at the gate.

"Please come in." I allowed gaily.

"Sir, it was really one of the most interesting day full of fun and frolic here in the Campus." He uttered with joyful expressions.

"Yeah, I also enjoyed the day. It was really a fun." I admitted.

"Sir, how about ma'am? She was leaning on you all the time." He said jokingly.

"Yeah, she is a nice lady; very cooperative and friendly." Putting of the main topic aside I said.

"No doubt she is. I have known her for the last two years, but I am talking about her inclination towards you." He spoke frankly. "The girls were saying that she talks much about you."

"Leave it Chirag. We should not throw dirt on or pollute genuine feelings. She's sui generis." I said forcibly.

"Wow, how lovely these roses are!" He exclaimed with surprise mixed with joy. "Nice collection, sir. The flowers are really intoxicating."

"Chirag! Be serious please. I have something very urgent to share." I muttered.

"Is it related to ma'am?" he made funny expressions.

"Please! No more kidding now." I said getting furious.

"Yes sir, I am damn serious and all ears now." He said resting his chin in both hands, eyes on me and ears on my words.

"Actually, I have neither plucked these flowers from the garden nor received as a token of love." I paused and resumed in a few seconds. "Every morning I find a fresh flower in my room. Now it may be a part of the hostlers' naughtiness I guess."

"No Sir! Never. If any student had a hand in it, I must have known. No one here dares to do anything without my assent." He said confidently.

"Then who can be behind it?" I said looking at the ceiling of my room.

Chirag kept on thinking for a few seconds and then spoke all of a sudden,

"Ma'am."

"What?" I asked out of surprise.

"Yes. You have made a very good impression on her from the first day." He said with confidence.

"Sir, do you sleep with all the exits shut?" he enquired.

"Actually, I am so careless that I leave either main or balcony gate open." I said irritatingly.

"Then it's ma'am only. No one else could dare to enter like this. Furthermore, her concern for you while dancing was the best evidence today." He alleged with a smile.

"I don't understand the mystery of the roses in my room, but the lady is too innocent to be allegated." I said firmly. "But I'm convinced that it's a way of showing love or affection irrespective of whosoever has put them."

The hostel bell rang, Chirag ran away guessing the Warden approaching in dormitory and taking the students for sports. Once more I was all alone to fight with some unsolved riddles in mind.

CHAPTER NINE

The Birthday Girl in Danger

I threw myself on the bed for relax. It being cold, I was creeping under quilt slowly. I had never been in a real serious relationship with a girl before. It had been a few hours only when she was in my arms, but in the interim I had thought of her thousand times. I often felt like I had known her forever and I found myself looking forward to seeing her, something that was so unusual for me.

I realized that I had feelings building for her. It was a wonderful experience for me, and I cherished the friendship that we were building in such a short time. But it was just a friendship, I had told myself. The evening became crisp and the leaves of roses in flower pot began to twist, a vivid color display amidst the evergreens.

The door was pushed all of a sudden with a bang. I got up and saw the current of fast blowing wind had come to see my well being. I bolted the door from within being rude to the unwanted guest of Chilling Wind.

It was useless to open the book and read between the lines so I thought of a better plan. I opened my balcony gate; leaned out of it and looked down; the puffs of wind were less harsh; the sports ground was enlivened with students at play; the hills were giving protection; the moon along with stars was viewing the Basket Ball match.

Chirag was a very good player of Basket Ball. Everyone loved to see him playing. I also accompanied the Moon and His family watching the sports. It had been a great fun and ecstatic pleasure to be on the ground among the students, but I confined myself for the fear of excessive chilled weather outside. To the contrary, exotic birds with feathers of gorgeous colors were unmindful to this chill.

I also sighted the small Birthday girl playing in a corner with her companions. She was scattering the pearls of laughter all around. Her presence was enough to illuminate the place.

Suddenly, some dark evil clouds devoured the happy Moon. I noticed the small girl shivering at play. She was not able to balance herself at times. She stopped and started gazing blankly. Now and then she twisted her neck and looked here and there. I was paralyzed and saw her helplessly going to the small gate of Sport Ground that opened in thick garden. She kept on moving and vanished from the sight. I flung out an arm unconsciously to stop her. The sports teachers were busy instructing the senior students. They had no notice of the birthday girl's endanger.

"The Birthday girl has disappeared." I shouted loudly coming out of my faint state, but the people on the ground floor couldn't listen. The chill of the wind had weakened my vocal cards and the auditory sense of the people on the ground.

I flung myself into motion after flinging the door wide open, a few seconds later, the door slammed behind me. I skipped madly on the stairs and the next moment at the bottom of stairs. I ran across the playground. I had forgotten all names but Chirag so I shouted loudly,

"Chirag, do follow me. Fast."

I saw the students throwing Basket Ball and rushing after me. I came out of the gate and found myself in utter darkness. I was baffled not to find any trace of the girl. In a flash, I heard a long mournful cry behind the shrubs and I rushed blindly among the thick plants. I got a narrow escape when I was almost on the ground. I heard Chirag saying, "sir what?"

"Chirag, Birthday girl is here. Search her fast." I whispered.

Soon I found her lying coiled under thick plants. When I took her in my arms, she was ice-cold. We rushed back to come out of the pall of terror in darkness. Chirag was holding my hand to control my excitement.

When we reached the playground, Chirag put his hand on the chest of the girl and reported to be alive. The sports were over. The students were being sent to the hostel. I requested Rishabh to call for the Doctor immediately. I was nervous with effete state. I requested Abhi to take her soon in Vidhya madam's room.

The uproar, outcry and panic had caused much upheaval in the Campus. Aanya had also come in slippers to inquire into. She caressed the girl in my arms. The girl was regaining consciousness so holding me tightly.

We led the girl to the room of her Warden; laid her in bed; covered her in quilt.

"Aanya, you please be with her in bed. She must not feel lonesome at present." I advised.

She entered the bed hurriedly and enfolded the sweet Birthday girl in her arms.

The medical attendant entered the room and observed the girl minutely. She had opened her eyes, but didn't respond to Doctor's questions.

"There's nothing to worry. She has caught cold. I have given the medicine. She'll be all right soon." The doctor advised before his departure.

The senior warden was not in the campus so Aanya was taking care of the girls in hostel.

When Birthday girl started feeling better, the sports teacher and the wardens of Boys hostel departed.

"Tanmay, please be here with ma'am by the time Warden comes." Rishabh said. He also took Chirag with him.

I was so upset by the bygone happening that my heart was still galloping behind ribs. On my gentle touch, the birthday girl opened her eyes; saw us sitting; got up quickly and hugged me tightly. I also pressed her close to my heart and made her believe that now she was quite safe with us. I tickled her slowly to ask what happened really. I let her sit comfortably with the support of pillow against the wall. I and Aanya were sitting one on each side holding her hands.

Her dark eyes flashed and darkened nearly to purple. A sob escaped and the words caught in her throat. I was surprised by the wave of emotion that swept over me. I again gave her a close hug to make her feel comfortable. When her pounding heart took its normal speed, she disclosed something that gave us goose pimples. We held our breaths and listened.

"Sir, I was busy playing with my friends. I was so happy, but all of a sudden I saw a shadow calling me and touching me from all around. The figure was very strange to look at so I kept staring at it. In a few seconds, I lost my senses and started following it. The shadow took me in the thick garden and disappeared. Some horrible faces started dancing and I was scared. I turned to run out, but I was struck and fell down unconscious." Her voice trailed off. Bright pink circles had erupted on her cheeks. She was embarrassed by what she said. She raised her sad, red-rimmed eyes to me. Tears rolled down her swollen cheeks.

I patted her hair gently and tried my best to comfort her.

A sob escaped Aanya's throat. She changed her side, came to me, gasped and squeezed my arm. Her hand was suddenly ice-cold. I too felt scared of her story about the shadow that reminded me of the horrible dream I saw the last night. It was also the shadow that led me to the sinister caves full of human debris that manifested carnage.

CHAPTER
TEN

Teacher's Day Celebration

It was 5th of September. The heart had started pounding since I opened my eyes. The whole night I kept practicing dance with her in my dream. Her dark eyes flashed and seemed inviting me.

"Today we have to dance together so I can't afford to get late." I talked to myself.

I kicked off the heavy quilt and started to climb out of bed. My legs were tangled in the sheet, and I nearly fell. But I caught my balance.

The curtains fluttered over me as I dove to the open window and peered out. A gust of wind ruffled my thick brown hair. The surprise of the previous nights had faded from my face, replaced by a smile.

Today, there was something special; something very special. I had handed over my DG cam to Chirag already to catch every moment of our dance, and ordered him to remain quite close to the stage.

I dressed up myself in best attire and turned to leave, but I stopped when my eyes landed on the fresh rose at the edge of the table. Today, I felt glad for the first time to find rose in my room. Moreover I had decided to ask Aanya, "Why she places a rose stealthily in my room every day?"

I felt the entire room perfumed with the smell of beautiful roses. I had a pleasant glance at all the flowers kept in the vase on the table. They were still fresh.

I viewed my reflection many times and hurried down the stairs. Then I made my way along the garden to the Reception.

"Happy Teacher's day" was flowing from every pair of lips with a genial smile. An atmosphere of warmth and geniality was prevailing in the entire Campus. The teachers could be seen embracing and hugging the students enthusiastically. The stream of love and affection had drowned every soul all over.

The students had taken the charge of comparing the performances. The event started with the best wishes to the principal and the teachers. The lady teachers of junior school conducted the Assembly in school uniform that inflated the heart of the students with joy. The events continued and I waited eagerly every moment with my heart in my eyes for the Dance event.

The participants of the Dance event had collected backstage in a hall. When the event was announced to be performed, we entered the stage hand in hand. The music had already started so we moved with well organized steps. While performing I had forgotten Aanya's touch at all. What I kept in mind was to dance well and prove that her training had not gone in vain. I felt a sort of enthusiasm, caring her at every step so that she might not fall. The music had started going in background so we made a circle and got down thanking the audience.

The uproar in the audience had proved that we had done astoundingly well. The round of applause was audible for many moments. We had reached the hall, the venue decided to meet after the performance. All the participants were greeting one another. In this breathing spell, I was enfolded in arms tightly with a jerk.

"Tanmay, you are fabulous. You are a darling." Aanya had embraced me passionately after the grand success of the event. Now started a big round of applause in the hall; the participants had made a circle around us. They all were appreciating our performance and the new built friendship. We were locked in a passionate embrace.

She loosened her arms; I let her go; her eyes were brimming over with flood of joy and love. I went forth; cupping her face in both hands; raised her head and said with love: "You are gorgeous and angelic. I'm glad to have you as my friend."

The final announcements were on; we held our breaths.

"The award of the best performance of the day goes to "Aanya and her Group".

Again I heard a round of applause from the students. This time they all made whoopee and enfolded us tightly. We were ten shadows with one soul.

She held my left hand tightly; dragged me to the stage. Next moment we were standing on the stage with our group at our back. She received the Trophy with both hands and shared it during photo session by letting all of us touch it and have our photo clicked.

I guess I really lucked out when I met her. I felt a surge of love and desire for her.

CHAPTER ELEVEN

Euphoria at Night

The whole day had passed cheerfully. It was so full of fun and frolic. I felt so good that I wanted to sing and shout.

I finished my tea to feel warm against the rising chill of the evening. I shivered as I pulled on a flannel nightshirt. My room was cold and drafty. But I moved to the window and pulled it open a few inches to have fresh air.

Outside the front window, I saw a bright half moon rising over the bare trees. The tree branches bent and swayed. Wind rattled the old windowpanes.

A cold breeze fluttered the curtains around me. I backed away from them, turned off the lamp on my bed table, and climbed under the heavy quilt on my bed.

I shut my eyes and tried to clear my mind. I was just drifting off to sleep when I heard footsteps in the Corridor...and then my bedroom door swung open.

As the door opened, light from the hallway swept over the roses on the table. With the moonlight entered a slim human figure. Her hair was a gray mop gathered into tiny knots and clamped in place with metal curlers.

Hurried glance I saw that the door was shut, and horror! The shadow threw itself heavily on the bed, outside the clothes, and lies there, slim and swart, in the white gleam of the moon that treacherously died away after showing so much to affright, and sinks into dull darkness. There was now no light left, though the big two eyes like headlights yet glowed with a ruddy gleam like the eyes of wild beasts.

I felt scared to death. I tried to speak, to scream wildly for help; my mouth was parched, my tongue refused to obey. I could not utter a cry.

I strove to pray aloud as there rushed on my memory a flood of weird legends—the dreaded yet fascinating lore of my childhood. I had heard and read of the spirits of the wicked men forced to revisit the scenes of their earthly crimes—of demons that lurked in certain accursed spots—of the ghoul and vampire of the East, stealing amidst the graves they rifled for their ghostly banquets; and then I shuddered as I gazed on the blank darkness where I knew it lay. The shadow stirred and touched me. I drew myself from it, shrinking away in loathing and terror of the evil thing—what, I knew not, but felt that something horrible was at hand.

My hair bristled; my eyeballs seemed starting from their sockets; the damps of a great anguish were on my brow. My heart labored as if I were crushed beneath some vast weight. Sometimes it appeared to stop its frenzied beatings, sometimes its pulsations were fierce and hurried; my breath came short and with extreme difficulty, and I shivered with cold yet I feared to stir.

"Hello Tanmay! Don't panic. I'm Aanya." The shadow came to life, and breaths to me.

A strange, snickering laugh escaped her lips.

"Hi! I was really scared." I said shuddering in bed as I was in least clothes.

Now the beauty of her face was enough to lighten the room yet I felt formal.

"Switch on the light. The board is there behind the gate. I can't get up because I have worn very less clothes." I spoke feeling shy.

"There is no need to switch on the light. The moonlight is enough." She spoke softly.

The gray light flooding in from the window made her look like a beautiful statue. She sat on the edge of my bed; placed her cold white hand on my warm hand; and communicated her love and affection through lips.

"How was it?" she asked in a whisper.

"It was delicious." My lips vibrated.

Shivering, we pulled the quilt up to our chin and it was large enough to cover two-in-one. Silvery moonlight washed in through the window. The curtains fluttered softly.

Her dark curls fell damply over her face. Her hands were clenched into tight fists in the bed. The sheets felt scratchy. And the heavy quilt smelled of mothballs.

She felt the tension in my body increasing and was helpless to prevent the same anxious straining in her own. Her fingers slipped into my hair; her deceptive strength holding my mouth to hers. The tip of my tongue brushed by the curve of her lower lip, and I caught her breath. My tongue began tasting her, outlining the delicate contours of her lips, and then parting the willing petals to explore the sweet secret recesses.

I was deaf, dumb and immune to the world abroad. All I could do was to taste the rose-scented skin. We didn't talk; she didn't accuse me of anything or tell me I was being childish. We lay there facing the rising storm and I simply enjoyed her closeness. Finally, she looked at me in her quiet way and smiled her black eyes warm as she said, "None of it matters to me. Only you matter to me."

CHAPTER TWELVE

An Encounter with the Shadow

The room was warm; the light was on and I had already closed the window. We had emptied the cups of coffee and placed on the table beside the roses in vase.

She was wearing my Jacket and sitting on sofa across the table. There was charm in her grace. She smiled like a flower in full bloom. She looked at the roses, "Wow! How lovely flowers! Nice collection!" she exclaimed with surprise. Her mouth quivered in the suspicion of a smile.

I climbed out of bed with a smile on face, "Don't keep it a mystery, please. This is the happiest day of our life. Let me know if it's you who have placed these flowers in my room?" I asked going near her.

"How can I keep the flowers in your room? We have known each other just now." she shrugged petulantly. "You are kidding. Aren't you?" she asked anxiously.

"I'm not kidding. Believe me. Each word of mine is as true as our friendship. I trust you so don't feel that I'm blaming you." I was upset.

There was a small silence in all the corners of the room. She composed her face into a calm smile and passed an affectionate smile at me.

"What happened? Don't get nervous." She got up and sat by me taking my head on her lap. "Now tell me. What's the mystery of these flowers?" she asked caressing my head with right hand fingers.

There was something in her cool and loving touch that proved her truthfulness. I felt very domesticated.

I got up; made myself sit comfortably against the wall with the support of a pillow. The room was warm enough with her presence so I didn't feel the need to slip in bed.

When I parted my lips, my tongue felt stiff and my lips were unable to form the words.

"I'm sorry if my words have hurt you.... Actually, since the very first morning of my arrival here, I have been receiving a rose daily. In the first couple of days, I was anxious to know who's this much interested in me. First, I felt it may be the naughtiness of the students, but Chirag came and clarified that no student has done this. Then he suggested me your name. Though I didn't believe him, but when I became pally with you, I stopped thinking of flowers in my room." I uttered and lost in a blank world.

"Now when it's clear that you also know nothing about the roses, the question arises then who's there behind all this?" I said irritatingly.

"Since the day I'm here, I have always noticed something scary in the breeze. And that bloody gardener! His words aggravate my panic." I continued.

My words had chilled her; she looked worried to see the signs of anxiety on my face and the tormenting dilemma I was passing through.

"Tanmay, please, don't get excited. It's so simple. There's nothing scary behind all this. You just take rest. Tomorrow we'll discuss it in detail and very soon we'll find the real culprit behind all this." She comforted me like a true friend.

I didn't try to kiss her again. I just held her, almost fiercely, my lips at her ear, my whispering almost unintelligible.

"I wish I'd known you long ago," I murmured. "I want to know you now."

She smiled; pushed me affectionately.

"Now you just lie down; cover yourself nicely; dream of me." she said kidding.

"We'll meet in the morning. And one thing more—though I know nothing about these red roses, I'll bring you a rose tomorrow in the morning—but not stealthily." She fluttered her eyelashes at me and went away.

I knew it would take me a long time to fall asleep. No matter how hard I tried, I couldn't shut off my mind.

I lay thinking that I won't be able to relax—until I learn the truth about that Gardener.

I had hardly had a wink of sleep when I felt something unusual, I got up. I took a quick peep through my window. I couldn't see anything unusual except the shivering moon traveling in biting chill.

I don't know what was going inside me that led me to open the balcony gate and peep out. My eyes went with surprise to see the fanatic gardener moving in the garden at such late hours.

"Why the hell he's out there when everyone has been chilled by the icy wind?" I pondered. "Today I'll definitely find out the truth about him."

I pulled on a clean pair of black lower and a bright yellow wool sweater; went running to the hostel dormitory and asked Chirag to follow me. He was wearing his night suit. He took his blanket; wrapped himself and we hurried down to follow the Hillbilly.

The cold, fresh air made our cheeks tingle. The bright moon, high in clear blue sky, felt kissing on our skin.

On the ground floor, I glanced around frantically, searching for a hiding place. Finding nothing we ducked out of sight behind the assembly platform, and saw Hillbilly going to the gate which the birthday girl disappeared through. Our doubts were getting intense and suspense more heightened.

Hillbilly was a bit careless as he had never expected someone to follow him. He disappeared soon behind the shrubs. We came out and moved to that gate stealthily.

We had condescended from teacher and student to spy on the gardener.

We moved along the wall in the dark or shaded portions so that no one could see us. In the meantime, we heard someone in the stairs.

Chirag was puzzled to feel that the Warden might have seen his vacant bed, and would be searching for him. I squeezed his hand not to care. I'll tackle all this. He calmed down and we also disappeared in the shrubs.

It was so dense that we couldn't see what was there on the next step. Moreover we had to take care so that our moving might not create stir among the leaves. We were holding the hand of each other so that in time of need we could help each other.

The other reason was the fear of unknown. We didn't know what we were following and what we were going to come across. We had the least idea that if something unusual happened, how we would tackle there.

"But one thing is sure that nothing bad can happen to Chirag till I am breathing." I thought.

The next moment I clapped my hand on Chirag's mouth to keep from gasping and suspended my breath. The entire body locked in horror when I saw Hillbilly shaking a tree and talking to it. There was someone skulking behind the bushes. My heart pounded as I eavesdropped on his blubbing.

His voice was muffled enough to reach our ears, but it was sure that there must be someone behind the tree. It being dark, we couldn't see him.

Then followed Hillbilly's chuckling laugh that froze our very marrow and the gnashing of teeth as in demoniac frenzy; and then a wailing moan, and this was succeeded by silence.

I rested my frozen lips on left ear of Chirag and whispered "Chirag let's run and catch who this moron is talking to?"

Chirag tightened his body; spread himself. I could feel his confidence through his tightening wrist. But again panic and the fear of unknown sent a chill down my spine.

We knew nothing what we were aiming at? If it be a man with some sharp weapon in his hands, how would he react to our armless assault? If Chirag got hurt, what answer would I give to the Warden and School authorities? If something catastrophic resulted in my case then what would happen with my....

"I should drop the idea." I decided.

I kept looking at Hillbilly suspiciously. I began to feel cramped hiding under the shrubs. My knees ached. My back ached. In extreme chilled, my right hand had fallen asleep.

"This was a big mistake." I thought. "I won't be able to solve the Hillbilly's riddle at all. We shouldn't be hiding in here spying on him. We had better enjoyed the warmth of heavy quilt".

In a couple of minutes, he turned back and passed very close to us. We froze with terror so clamped our eyes. He had almost scared us to death.

We'd been holding our breaths the whole time so we let it out in a loud whoosh. I raised both hands to my cheeks. My skin was burning hot.

He passed taking long steps. We followed him from behind. This time we were not walking together.

I was keeping an eye on the front while Chirag holding my hand was looking back and moving at a snail's pace.

When we had reached very close to the play ground, we saw Hillbilly going to the Employee's residence where he lived.

He was far from us so we could easily walk across the play ground without being seen. We had hardly come out of the shrubs when we saw a shadow moving across the playground. We lay hid again and watched minutely where the shadow went.

The ground rocked and bobbed beneath us. I shut my eyes for a jiffy, waiting my legs to stop trembling.

Unfortunately the shadow entered the hall and vanished into thin air. We were afraid if anything wrong might not happen with students sleeping in the hostel.

The next idea struck the mind lest the shadow should be going to place the rose in my room. I shuddered at the thought.

The next moment I asked Chirag to unwrap the Blanket. I took it and ran with blanket in my hands and Chirag followed me.

The shadow was nowhere on the stairs. Our bodies were shaking with fear or chilled. Know not what.

I reminded of 'fools rush in where angels fear to tread'. I wanted to smile, but the smile froze on my lips when I saw the shadow moving in Corridor on our floor.

I spread the blanket with both hands and stuck against a wall beside the stairs on my floor. Chirag sat down behind me. The moment shadow came close to us; we attacked it; covered in blanket; muffled the voice and dragged into my room.

Fortunately, it was a human figure not a spirit otherwise it would have disappeared.

"Check the hands whether there is a rose." I spoke after a long time.

Chirag checked both the hands. There was nothing.

"Switch on the light and close the door so that whoever is there may not run away." I asked Chirag and he followed.

"Hold both the hands tightly and don't leave. I am unveiling the shadow." I said with confidence.

"Ready?" I whispered.

"Ready," he whispered back.

I was very happy to think that today I had succeeded in my mission. I let out a quiet sigh of relief, and then shot Chirag a warning glance.

"It was this shadow only whom Hillbilly was talking in the garden. Moreover this shadow is the one who keeps awaking at such late hours and disturbs the people like us by placing flowers in rooms." I kept blubbing while unveiling it.

"Okay," I uttered in last moments, "One...two...three."

The veil was off.

I had a self-satisfied smirk on my face.

Chirag had fallen on the floor; he had left the shadow's hands; he was lying prostrate folding his hands in worship.

I went stone cold. My hands shook, but I gripped the weird shadow tightly. When the shadow turned its face to me, I also collapsed on the floor folding my hands in prayer. I was scared out of my skin.

Actually we had committed a mistake. It was not a shadow but Aanya, who had seen us hurrying downstairs. It was she whose steps we heard on the stairs when we were in the Garden.

She caught my hands; helped me to get up; enfolded me in her arms. Chirag closed the door after him and ran away to think *two is company three is none.*

I was full of regret and remorse. She separated my both hands; put them across her waist and pushed me on the bed. A strange, snickering laugh escaped her lips. She held me in a warm embrace.

Outside the front window, the bright half moon was rising over the bare trees. The tree branches were bending and swaying. Wind was rattling the old windowpanes.

A cold breeze fluttered the curtains around me, but the storm inside was more powerful than any storm outside.

CHAPTER THIRTEEN

Blood on Windowpanes

The whole day the freezing rain kept pounding the windows and pouring in buckets confining the students and teachers in their respective rooms.

I spent a dreary afternoon studying in my room. When I couldn't bear, I tossed my books onto my bed and ran out of the room.

The building was cold and damp. I pulled a heavy wool sweater two T-shirts, but I still felt chilled.

A sweet cool wind was blowing and it was still drizzling outside. I spread arms to refresh myself, and started strolling in the corridor crooning romantically. There I heard someone climbing upstairs hurriedly and noisily.

I kept gazing in the stairs. In a few seconds, I sighted Abhinav, a close friend of Chirag. He had a puzzled look on his face. Beads of perspiration stood out on his forehead. There were fearful expressions in his body language as if something wrong had happened with him or he had committed some wrong.

When I saw him looking at me helplessly, I couldn't resist myself reaching him and enquiring into the matter.

"What happened, Abhinav? Why are you looking so haggard and drawn?" I asked getting restless.

"Sir, I'm sorry. I'm sorry to say, but your Chirag is really in trouble." he uttered nervously.

"What happened? Tell me fast if there is anything serious? Is he hurt or encountered something unlikable?" I asked holding his both the hands.

He was still looking at the floor. His body was quite loose that raised my anxiety for the safety of Chirag. I darted into my room, a jacket on. I stormed out of the room and crashed the door shut behind.

"Sir, listen to me. It's urgent." Abhinav cried at my back.

I stopped and rushed back, shook him exerting force.

"Why don't you tell me what had happened with my Chirag?" I was very near to shed tears.

"Sir, there is nothing to fear. He is quite well, but the problem is...."

"What's the problem? Speak up." I said getting angry.

"Sir, actually, it being a holiday today, there were no classes. Consequently, Chirag couldn't meet Meghana who was in your dance group. She is a good friend of him. Today he went with me to her hostel, but couldn't meet her. He, therefore, climbed to the roof with the support of a ladder. He, was caught red handed talking to Meghana in her balcony. When I saw him in trouble, I have directly come to you rushing. I know only you can bring him out of danger.... If Rishabh Sir came to know, he'll expel both of us." He stopped and again started surveying the ground with heavy heart.

I felt pretty relaxed to hear that Chirag was alright though he was in difficulties due to his childish pranks.

"Who is the teacher on duty in Girls' Hostel?" I asked softly making him feel relaxed.

"Sir, Aanya ma'am is on duty there. She has caught him and handed to the Gatekeeper." He informed looking at me.

A pink smile ran on my face to think the pink weather supporting the romance but pink lady not.

"Don't worry. You go to your dormitory and take rest. Moreover, don't tell anyone about all this. OK." I said comforting him.

When Aanya came to know that I had come to Girls' Hostel. She comprehended everything in no time. She came to me wearing a broad smile on her face.

"Hi! Tanmay, you must have come for your Chirag if I'm not wrong." She chirped happily with naughtiness in her eyes.

"No! Not at all! Actually, the weather is so congenial; I couldn't resist myself having a look at your pretty face." I said with love in my eyes.

"Then you'll be punished for being so casual with a lady teacher that too in Girls' Hostel." She exhibited the rising naughtiness in her eyes.

"If you want to punish, then punish the weather that has generated such warm and wild feelings in innocent hearts. Why do you hold me responsible?" I replied with equal naughtiness in my eyes.

"OK. I've understood everything well now." She shouted for the Gatekeeper and asked him to let Chirag go.

Chirag saw me at the gate so kept his eyes staring the ground and ran away saying, "Sorry ma'am; sorry sir." We burst into a soft and sweet laughter.

All the resident teachers had collected in the Cafeteria and were enjoying themselves. They were cutting jokes. The whole environment was full of fun and frolic.

The hostlers were taking refreshment standing in queue. They had to attend Prep Classes.

In the meantime, a student came rushing. The blood was spurting from his right hand. With the left hand, he had squeezed the right to prevent the gushing blood.

All the teachers stood up seeing the pitiable condition of the boy and the signs of pain on the face. When the boy came quite close to us, I recognized him that he was the same boy who gave me a kiss in the Dining Hall. My heart started pounding out of affection for him. I flinched at the sight of the blood. My throat dried up.

"Where were you? How did you get hurt?" Abhi growled squeezing his other arm.

"When all the students are here, where had you gone and why?" He narrowed his eyes at the boy.

The boy was not in a state to explain. He was writhing in pain; his eyes watering.

"Please Sir, don't get angry. He needs immediate help. Where is our first aid box?" Aanya suggested.

I moved close to the boy as I was feeling his pain in my heart.

"Leave your hand and show me the injury." I asked.

He let his hand go. He had a big cut at two three places and his all fingers were badly injured. The skin had come off at many places. I felt that his hand might have been chewed by some wild animal.

The Guard was sent to take First Aid Box from the hostel.

"How did you get hurt? Speak up." The Warden demanded, spitting the words on his face.

"Actually sir, the sweeper has collected many broken glasses in the corner there near the Assembly platform. When we were coming from the hostel, I felt the need to pee. As I ran up the corner, my foot slipped and I fell. The broken glasses lying pricked on my hand all over." He interpreted.

Even though his narration was appealing, I felt it like a tall story. I could hardly believe him.

"You are no less. Can't you relieve yourself in the hostel? Why did you go behind the bush?" Abhi enquired.

"Sorry sir, the pressure was mounting up. I couldn't handle for long. In hostel, I didn't pay much attention." He spoke writhing in pain.

First Aid Box had reached by that time so, I dipped a cotton ball in spirit and cleaned the blood clots around the injuries. His hand was seriously injured. The cuts on hand immediately needed to be stitched.

The Warden also felt the need to be attended by the Doctor. But it being a rainy day, the doctor denied driving the car at night.

Consequently, we had to send a car to pick up the doctor from his home that was 10 km away. Rishabh got ready. The car allotted for Resident Teachers was on the driveway.

"Tanmay, you please take care. I'll come back within half an hour." He requested.

"Sure sir, I'm here. You don't worry." I replied.

"Please take care. Drive slow. It's slippery on the road. "I shouted loudly when Rishabh was taking the car toward Gate No. 2.

He waved his hand and was out of sight in a few seconds.

I applied the lotion on his injuries. It was biting his open injuries. He was writhing in pain.

When the boy felt a bit relieved, I decided to take him to my room. He was staggering to his feet and was reluctant to go there.

"Sir, don't take me there in the hostel, I can't manage to walk." He retorted.

"What happened? I'll support you. Come along with me. I'll not leave you alone. You'll sit with me in my room." I relaxed him.

I took the boy in my room; made him sit comfortably; caressed his hair.

"Now tell me exactly. How did you get hurt?

"Sir, I respect you a lot and feel very homely with you so I'll not hide anything from you." He spoke softly.

"Actually I was not there with the students when they left the hostel for Cafeteria. I was sleeping in my bed. No one noticed me." he said leaning towards me.

I could easily smell the lurking danger and trouble behind his words.

"The warden went with the students. He left me sleeping like a baby. I was dreaming of my home. I was coaxed to wake up. When I woke up, I felt the gentle touch on my face. There was someone cupping my face and whispering in my ears. Get up. You are late. All your friends have gone for refreshment. I opened my eyes; I could see very vaguely. It was like a SHADOW. I could see its back only. I was puzzled and scared."

He started gasping. I poured some water in glass gave him to drink. He drank one draught and felt relieved.

His words were coated with the innocent truth that needed no evidence.

"The shadow was a male figure or female?" I asked.

"Sir, I can't remember well. The voice was soft enough for a man. The gait was unusual for a lady."

"OK. You leave it. Speak further." I said.

"I saw the Shadow disappearing from my room without opening the gate. I was shocked. I rushed to the gate and found it latched from outside. I was weeping, crying and thumping the gate, but there was no one to listen. The fear of the shadow was haunting me all the more." The boy spread himself on the sofa; looked here and there.

"Sir, I tried tugging the doorknob with all my strength. Then I tried to batter the door open with my shoulder. I failed in all the way." He kept speaking.

"I heaved with all my might but still couldn't budge it. I was scared enough so I couldn't wait for someone to come and open it. I therefore, thought of breaking the glass panel of the door. I made a frantic dash to find something that can break the panel."

"Finding nothing, I started throwing my books on the panel, but I couldn't break it. In a fitful fever, I struck my fist against the glass panel. It broke into pieces, but my hand was badly injured. I saw the skin had come off at many places, but I didn't feel the pain of injury. I put my hand from the hole in panel and tried to unlatch the door, but the sharp end of the broken panel peeled off my hand's skin again. I started feeling a severe pain all over the hand." He wiped the tears of fear from his face and looked to and fro.

"The door opened with a loud and painful cry as the spikes on the panel felt piercing my hand. There was nothing but blood at the gate. I was already in a state of panic, but the ghastly scene of blood pouring out of cuts made me faint. I rushed downstairs."

"But...but again I felt the voice of the shadow at my back. It was asking me to stop and go slow. I was too horrified to look back. I stopped only when you teachers came into my view." His voice was trembling in fright. He took a deep breath and tried to slow his racing heart. His chest heaved up and down. His breath came in hoarse wheezes.

I grabbed his injured part with trembling hand. My hand shook so hard, I nearly dropped it.

My eyes bulged wide in fear and then thousands of questions flooded my mind. I was out of my wits. All the previous unusual, scary, bizarre and weird happenings flashed through my mind. The next moment, I heard footsteps in the corridor; the door was flung open. It was a gust of wind. I let out a long sigh of relief.

My heart was thudding in my chest and my head spinning. I raised both hands to my cheeks. My skin was burning hot.

In a couple of minutes, the doctor entered my room and attended the student. I got up; put a blank expression on my face and tried to act casual as I walked out of the room.

CHAPTER FOURTEEN

The Angel of Death in My Room

The doctor had returned and the student had moved to dormitory. The power supply was cut. It was dark all around. I was left strolling on my knees.

As I entered my room, I thought I heard something stir in the room. But I was determined to have no more panics, and resolutely shut my eyes to this slight and transient noise, which had nothing unnatural in it. On a stormy night needs no spirits to disturb it.

A very good room it was, after all, now that the green damask curtains were drawn, candles burning on the mantle-piece, and the various familiar articles of cosmetics arranged as usual. The bed, too, looked peaceful and inviting—a pretty queen size bed, not at all the gaunt funereal sort of couch which haunted apartments generally contain.

A sort of dread of being alone led me longing to keep some human being near me possessed me. I thought of Aanya and her soft touch. Finding her not close to me, I took a dislike to the rich curtains, the tapestry cushions, the dingy pictures—everything. I hated the room. I felt a temptation to put on a shawl, run, half-dressed, to her room, and say 'I have come for shelter.' But she must be asleep, I thought, and I could not be so unkind as to wake her. I said my prayers with unusual earnestness and a heavy heart. I extinguished the candles, and was just about to lay my head on my pillow, when the idea seized me that I would fasten the door. The candles were extinguished, but the moonlight was amply sufficient to guide me.

I crossed my bedroom to the window which looked out over the hills. There was bright moon so the night was profoundly pleasant here away from the city noises. The sight seemed to reassure me and I sprawled across the big bed.

I had played the past event cool. The sweet face of Aanya; her pretty caring and loving nature, did a favor—diverted my thoughts from brooding unnecessarily.

I sank back on my pillow and waited for my heart to stop thudding so hard in my chest. I raised my black eyes to the ceiling, staring at the cool witness of it.

The electricity resumed; the room lighted up and I let my attention touch lightly on the roses on the table. Then I allowed my glance to wander here and there.

Suddenly, my heart, literally, did a flip-flop, and I thought I was the victim of a hallucination. I was on the point of dropping asleep, when I heard an owl hooting in the deodar outside—no unaccustomed sound, but harsh and melancholy generally taken as ill-omen—a note as the vulgar declare to herald a death in the family.

This was a fancy I had never shared; but still I could not help feeling that the owl's mournful hooting was sad, and expressive of terror as if something evil and unwanted were abroad.

I lay awake for a good while, watching the red roses in the flower vase. I switched off the light and there was ink-black darkness in my bedroom. I was quiet now, and more composed. Then I cooled my heels for a few sweet winks of sleep.

In a flash, I shuddered to find some soft touches at the soft parts of my body. I opened and strained my eyes; they could not penetrate the obscurity that shrouded the room. In a moment several distinct trains of thought, like any-colored strands of thread twining into one, became palpable to my mental vision.

I waited. My heart beat on; quicker, more sudden grew its pulsations, as a bird in a cage might flutter in presence of the hawk. And then I heard a sound, faint, but quite distinct, the jingling of bangles, the rattling of anklets! I ventured to lift my head from the pillow. Dim and uncertain as the light was, I saw the curtains of my bed shake, and caught a glimpse of something beyond, a darker spot in the darkness.

This confirmation of my fears did not surprise me so much as it shocked me. I strove to cry aloud, but could not utter a word.

The sofa creaked and shook. This was no phantom, no air-drawn specter. But its very solidity, its palpable presence, was a million times more terrible. I felt that I was in the very grasp of what could not only affright but cause harm; of something whose contact sickened the soul with ghastly fear. I made a desperate resolve: I glided from the bed; seized the pillow under my head, threw it around me, and tried to grope, with extended hands, my way to the door. My heart beat high at the hope of escape. But I had scarcely taken one step before the moaning was renewed—it changed into a threatening growl that would have suited a wolf's throat, and a hand clutched at my sleeve. I stood motionless. The muttering growl sank to a moan again, bangles sounded no more, but still the hand held its gripe of my wrist, and I feared to move. It knew of my presence, then. My brain reeled, the blood boiled in my ears, and my knees lost all strength, while my heart panted like that of a deer in the wolf's jaws. I sank back, and the benumbing influence of excessive terror reduced me to a state of stupor.

Notwithstanding this silence, by some intuition I knew that I had not been deceived by a dream, and felt certain that I was not alone.

Then I heard the curtains rattling and the bed shrieking. I shrank back against the wall as I heard someone approaching.

Then I heard a whisper. "*S – a – r – t –h –a –k...*"

I uttered a short, terrified whimper; felt choked out and started backing away, my eyes wide with fright.

My heart skipped a beat. "Go away," I said. My voice muffled as I buried my head in the duvet. The eerie voice calling was not that of Aanya playing a prank. I didn't know this voice.

"Chirag, help me!" I gave a loud cry of fright and then closed my eyes tightly.

When my full consciousness returned I was sitting on the edge of the bed, shivering with cold, and barefooted. All was silent, but I felt that my sleeve was still clutched by an unearthly visitant. The silence lasted a long time.

I switched on the light. Hideous visions passed before the aching eyes that I dared not close, but which gazed ever into the dumb horror of my room.

I pictured the bygone event in every abhorrent form which an excited fancy could summon up: now as a skeleton; with hollow eye-holes and grinning, fleshless jaws; now as a vampire, with livid face and bloated form, and dripping mouth wet with blood.

I had heard of specter and fiend from my grandfather, but this creature was too real, too foul a thing of earth, to be a paranormal creature. And then the cold prevailed, and my teeth chattered, and shivering ran through me, and yet there was the damp of agony on my bursting brow. Some instinct made me snatch at a shawl or cloak that lay on a chair within reach, and wrap it round me.

I was shaken to the core at the thought whether the horror was a fevered dream, a hallucination of sickness or an airy phantom.

Hours fled by, and I remained like a statue of ice, rigid and mute. There was nothing there, I assured myself. My breathing returned to normal.

"You're making up more ghost stories. You're scaring yourself again ...you're bored and lonely, and so you're letting your imagination run away with you." I pacified my restless heart.

I couldn't fall asleep. I sat on my bed and tossed my pillow into the air. I watched the numbers slowly click by in the clock on the wall.

I even slept, for I remember that I started to find the cold gray light of an early winter's day was on my face, and stealing around the room from between the heavy curtains of the window.

CHAPTER FIFTEEN

Ecstasy Under Shivering Moon

It was a pleasant night with a fresh breeze blowing from the northeast. The Moon along with hundreds of stars had already appeared in the royal blue sky. Due to shiver in breeze, he was trying to hide behind the hills.

We had promised to meet on the top floor of our building after dinner. To keep my promise I left my room and went upstairs.

Aanya had already reached there. She was leaning on the terrace and mooning about me. The lights flowing from all the sides in the hills were looking like glimmering jewels studding the dark green of the mountains.

She had not noticed that she had an audience. A tall slim young man in blue jeans, T-shirt and black leather bomber style jacket was at a distance with open admiration for her romantically beautiful face.

Her oversize sweet shirt, canvas cargo pants, shining Jacket in moonlight, and her blue grey eyes had a wonderfully deep and dreamy look about them like the stars in the sky. The two stars shining on her face were expressive of her every emotion and a very striking shade of moonlight.

To surprise her I stepped behind her and wrapped her up in a tight hug around the waist.

She shrugged. Her eyes crinkled in the corners as a shy smile crossed her face.

"I like your style. I wanted to be with you like this." She spoke romantically.

She took a turn and now she was in my arms with my lips on her forehead. She ran her fingers of one hand through my short hair.

"Dear, stop flirting." She spoke with naughtiness in her eyes.

As I kissed her, she had automatically closed her eyes, but as I lifted my mouth from hers, the sensation of deprivation was so intense that her eyes flew open.

The next moment, she got herself freed and ran to the other side of the roof.

I thought for a moment and ran after her. We chased each other around the water-tank on the roof tickling each other.

I caught her in my arms again.

"Why are you running away from me?" I asked gasping.

"I like puzzling you." She gasped out with a flicker of smile.

I could feel her breasts heaving.

"But why?" I asked rubbing my nose against hers.

She shrugged. Her eyes crinkled in the corners as a shy smile crossed her face.

"Just like that." She spoke while clinging to my back tightly in her arms.

It was a long moon-night. The hills all around had become frost glistening silent audience of our euphoria. Her sweet breath next to my face sent anxious messages through her body. She rested a hand on my chest and could feel the power in the tightening of my muscles at her touch. We enjoyed the shivering moon showering white light and very soon we were over the moon.

In the blink of an eye I had lifted her over the bend of my knees. We were only half aware of what we were whispering, too caught up in excitement to absorb every passing jiffy in exploring the heights of ecstasy.

I was torn between a desire to prolong this moment of intimacy, and a frightened urge to end it.

Her head was resting on my chest as she twisted half around so her arms could stay about my waist. Her heart was churning inside her making her restless. Conflicting emotions churned inside me also. My legs were pressing hers, our bodies melting together like two spoons resting cozily in a drawer.

I pressed her, my mouth gently brushing first her eyes and then her mouth, and then I parted my lips. Her eyes opened reluctantly.

A little while later, the gathering of dark clouds warned us of the approaching snow. It began with a slight fall first, followed by a heavier one. The snowflakes started kissing us all over.

She was deeply, crazily in love with me—I was the only thing that mattered and if I left her then she thought she might go crazy with the agony of losing me. I could feel her heart thudding heavily against her breastbone.

It was a novel sensation for her, and one that would once have terrified me, but which I now reveled in, knowing that I wasn't alone, that she shared my feelings.

Her cry of pleasure heightened by the sudden tension she felt within my grasp. Her control began to lose. The somberness in my eyes shattered, melting in the heat that sprang to life within us, my arms came round her, lifting her, my mouth hot as it touched her throat.

I tugged at one sleep of her top, then the other, and she helped me by leaning forward. She had put off her jacket. The front clasp of her camisole opened under skillful manipulations and the silky material was tossed aside forgetting chill against the warmth inside. Moonlight flickered over her bare skin as I adjusted her weight against one arm, leaving the other hand free to explore the beauty she had just exposed.

She was a small child in my arms, reclining there in my lap, confined by solid muscles. The movement of my hands against her skin was music translated into feelings. Her mouth parted eagerly to the gently insistent pressure of mine, her arms locking round me as gentleness gave way to passion. My hand roamed over her stomach, up through the deep shadowy hollow over the swelling ripeness of her breast.

Her body was slim, almost thin, but her breasts were full. Her hair brushed her shoulders shimmering under snowfall in the moonlight.

Her body trembled under my powerful hand, so gentle now, pushing, nudging, squeezing. I lifted her slightly and lowered my lips to her breasts pulling one rosy tip into the warmth of my mouth. I felt her tense beneath me as she fought to subdue the fierce clamor of need within her that demanded more, much more from me than mere tenderness.

Her fingers twined into my hair as she held me tightly to her breasts; then finally, wild with passion she urged my lips up to hers.

The tiny cries of pleasure she could no longer hold inside her chest seemed to fuel my passion as my mouth moved with fierce need from one aroused nipple to the other and then to the moist valley in between.

"Aanya!" I could barely speak. My words carried to her ear in short gasps. My fingers fumbled with the button of her....

Gladly she did my bidding, and in one smooth motion, she lay nude in my arms. I lifted her easily, then stood, turned and lowered her behind the water-tank-platform. My jacket was off before she could lift her eyes.

Her hands were trembling with chill. I knelt before her, took her hands between mine and kissed them. Our eyes met. There was no further need for words. I freed her hands, and she reached out for me, pulling me over her as she lay back on the mat of our put off clothes.

The sensations were unimaginable, inconceivably exquisite. She was helpless, at the mercy of unknown, ancient rhythms. My body covered her, a heavy, welcome gift she clung too passionately. The low, resonant sound of my voice enveloped her and stoked the unfamiliar fire that rose from deep within her body.

I moved with a tenderness I'd never felt before in all my life. My thoughts were ungovernable; I couldn't separate the vibrant sensations spiraling through my body from the feelings of joy in my heart, and I realized a vital emotional bond was being forged with each gentle motion my hands moved to form a cradle of protectiveness beneath her straining body as my desire mounted and took command.

Suddenly my mind whirled and reeled cursing my warm heart. I felt some trusted reluctance in my heart to deceive one who had reposed her staunchest faith in me. I felt powerless to belie the confidence Aanya had reposed in me.

How close we were then yet I broke off, appalled by our near indiscretion.... I anticipated her curiosity, but instead my expression went curiously blank, my arms instantly slackening to release her.

Our relationship, our feelings and trust of each other were too new for us to plunge into the heady waters of passion together yet.

CHAPTER SIXTEEN

A Mishap on the Terrace

The moments of ignited passions had passed and left us sitting against the water-tank-platform quietly together, easing slowly back into reality now. An apology was on my lips and in my heart. She was gazing me. I moved beside her.

"Aanya, are you all right?" I asked making her wear my jacket.

Two fingers silenced me. "Thank you for caring.... I want to have coffee." She spoke all of a sudden.

I felt shivery at her thought. It was quite late; the Cafeteria was already off.

"How can I manage the coffee for her here when we have nothing at hand?" I thought.

She was busy reading the tense expressions on my face and the struggle in my mind.

"There is a thermos placed on my table. It has two cups coffee. Wait, I'll fetch it in a few seconds." She spoke while making an attempt to get up.

I pulled her and made sit. I was happy to feel that her wish would not go unfulfilled now.

"You sit here. I'll get that in a few seconds." I assured her.

"If you are going, bring my shawl also. It's lying on my bed." She said while giving me the keys.

I took her keys and made a dash for her room. I took a few minutes to unlock her gate. Her room was warm like her kisses.

I was completely taken aback to see in. The room looked as if a tornado had swept through. Her dresser drawers had been pulled out and tossed onto the floor. Her clothes had been strewn everywhere.

The window curtains had been ripped off their rod. The window smashed; glass everywhere. The total chaos sent shivers down my spine.

With a shudder, I backed out of the frightening room and pulled the door shut. I had hardly locked her gate when I heard cries in her voice upstairs. I left the keys in the lock and ran upstairs. I reached breathing hard.

I ran blindly to her. She was terror stricken and on the verge of falling from the terrace. She screamed in a shrilling feminine voice and her eyes had rolled up, only the white of it could be seen.

I supported her. She collapsed in my arms. She was shaking with fear. Her expressions changed to bewilderment. I gave a cry of terror. Her arms and hands held me very tightly as though she was drowning and I was her savior. I was touching her face all over; placing several tiny kisses on her forehead; enfolding her tightly in my arms. So many frantic questions ran through my mind.

I kept rubbing my hands against hers unless she groaned and moaned. When she looked at me, her eyes were wild with terror; she hugged me tightly with all her might.

Her face tightened, as if she were in some acute pain. Her lips trembled.

"Ta . . . Tanmay." The words trembled from her lips giving way to the stream of warm tears rolling down her eyes.

She breathed deeply, gulping air. Finally, she clutched my shoulders and shoved her face right up close to mine.

"Aanya!" I cried restlessly. "What happened? Why are you so strained and unnerved?"

She was so scared to speak at the moment. Her words were staggering with the fear in her heart. I made her believe that I was with her so there was no cause to fear. She threw herself in my embrace like a little child. She gazed around in all directions, and then focused those blue crazy eyes on me. Then the words she uttered struck terror into our hearts and shook my body.

"Tanmay, there was someone who was trying to push me from the terrace. I couldn't see, but just felt the touch. It was scary. It has terrorized me to the core." Her eyes grew wide. She burst into tears. Her words were shaking with fear like her body.

I froze for a moment.

The moon had disappeared behind the hills; the dense pall of fog had covered us from all sides. A chill of fear passed through me. The constant fear of unknown was striking both of us. We were terribly shaken in fear of our lives.

I managed myself to stand on trembling legs and supported her to stand. She had no strength to walk on her own.

"Don't leave me alone...." Her voice trailed off. I could feel her face grow red.

I picked her up in my arms and took to my room as her room had already been ransacked. On reaching, I switched the room heater on to take the chill off the room.

Her loud scream on the terrace was just horrible; it was still giving me the creeps lying in bed beside her. I had a horrible suspicion that we had come to a wrong station. Furthermore it aroused the feeling that we couldn't trust the puffs of breeze even. The past experience had taught me that life could be very unfair.

She was all coiled up holding my shirt with both hands. She fell asleep clutching me to her while her features curved into an expression of ecstatic bliss.

Outside the front window, the bright half moon was rising over the bare trees. The tree branches were bending and swaying. Wind was rattling the old windowpanes. A cold breeze fluttered the curtains around me, but the storm inside was more powerful than any storm outside.

Moonlight streamed through the lace at the windows, silver-frosting Aanya's soft red curls, highlighting her body and her cheeks, still flushed with their passion.

CHAPTER SEVENTEEN

Accident on a Snowy Evening

The terrors of the night had passed. The morning presented the school among hills as a fantastic fairyland of white beauty. My hair still smelled of the odour on her hands. I woke up and felt a chill in the air. The chill grey dawn sent a quick message that it had been a night of heavy snowfall. The hills all around were snow covered and shining brightly. It spread a smile of satisfaction on the faces of boarders. The beautiful scenario all around was a rare piece of beauty to the Nature lovers.

While bathing, I heard some weird noises in my room. The door creaked open. Someone was shifting my table.

I kept asking, "Who is there?

"Aanya, is it you?" But I couldn't get any response.

I shuffled into the washroom for a towel and came out to see the destroyer of my peace. I scanned the room frantically. I wondered, gazing around the empty, silent living room. I was shocked and found myself in a real fit when I discovered my roses crushed on the table.

I felt scared and the chilling moments made my hair stand on end.

I rushed to the gate for a desperate search, but stopped and slunk back as I was wrapping a towel only around my waist and it was chilling cold outside. Distant creaks and groans echoed eerily along the dumb corridors. I was in an utter confusion regarding all this unusual happening with me. These evidences lent credence to the presence of paranormal force.

"Was it something paranormal? I asked to myself mopping the sweat from my forehead.

I was scared to death. The heart pounded fast and I jumped into bed and pulled the covers up to chin. Then I fluffed my pillows two-three times, trying hard to get comfortable. The warmth in bed made me feel a little safer.

I swung my legs out of bed. I took a deep breath. Then I lowered myself to the floor.

Though I was not the nervous type yet I felt a nervous disposition. The entire flower issue was shrouded in mystery and I was still helpless to know its source. To avoid confusion and depressed state of mind, I dropped the brainstorming puzzle to take up some other time. I got ready and went downstairs to have breakfast.

On the stairs my mind felt restless for Aanya so it led me to her gate. Her door stood slightly open. I poked my head in and checked out her bedroom.

By the dim light in her room, I could see her sitting in settee. Her pillow was lying on floor near her shoes. She wore a plain black dress and there was a high comb in her hair. Her face was pale and composed, with dark shadows under the eyes—eyes that somehow seemed to be as bottomless and black as the night. She was very beautiful, with firm white flesh and small hands and a full bosom swelling from the bodice of her dress. I could see the medallion she wore resting in the cleft of her breasts. She was in many ways more youthful than I had thought of her.

Soon I noticed her face changing colors and her hands waving in odd directions.

"Is she practicing dance steps?" I thought carefully.

"No! The dance steps are measured, supported by music and not odd at all. I answered my questions.

She gave jerks to her head and all her hair got spread on her face. What I saw chilled my blood. The scene was so full of panic that I could hardly stand to it. I stared at her, frozen with shock. I observed her moving to my side. Perhaps she had come to know that she had an audience at the gate. I stepped back from the door and ran away to have no more panic.

The cold waves blowing abroad made my skin shudder. Wet snow- drops from the trees blew into my eyes, blurring my vision.

The children were playing with the snow balls in the garden and the chilled weather had no effect on their warm spirits.

Over the breakfast table in Dining Hall, Chirag and other students wished "Good Morning!"

I gave a humorous smile to Chirag, who amused himself thinking of the Girls' Hostel Episode.

The teachers joined us in the Hall. They all were engaged in scholarly talks.

"Good Morning, Tanmay!" Rishabh came and sat by my side.

"Good Morning! I returned him with same geniality on my face.

"How is the life getting on here?" He asked showing friendliness.

"It's really a big fun" I answered hiding the expressions of anxiety on my face.

Then we started discussing the hostel matters and other important issues, but every time I felt the need to raise the last night's issue.

Since Rishabh was in a hurry so I postponed the matter to some other favorable occasion. It was he only in the Campus who was mature enough to answer my questions and satisfy the chain of queries in my agitated heart.

"Tanmay, we are going on picnic. Why don't you join us? You'll feel better. You'll love playing with the snow. Moreover, if you are with us, the responsibility will get shared and I'll feel a little lighter." He spoke placing his hand on my shoulder.

The wind-chill factor was a warning not to move out as I was not accustomed to such low temperature. Moreover I was nervous from the flower episode in the morning so half inclined not to go yet I nodded.

"Aanya is also going with the girls." He gave a broad smile and disappeared. I kept looking behind at him.

Mentioning of Tanya's name was enough to amuse my heart so, I was all smiles again. The next moment I reminded of the recent horror in her room. My blood stopped running for a while and the heart missed a beat.

"Tanmay Sir!" I felt a melodious choric voice at my back and blood circulation in veins.

When I looked behind, they all were wearing fur coats covering their heads also. Hence it was rather hard to recognize them all of a sudden. They all came close to me and stood in decent manner.

It was the group of students who participated in Dance.

"Sir, we are going on picnic. We'll feel happy if you accompany us. The wardens are very strict. If you are with us, we can enjoy much freely …you always help us so, we hope a favorable response." Meghana made a humble request coming quite close to me and unveiling her head. There was a pleased smile on her pink face.

She had really a nice smile. Actually, she was kind of cute. Today, she was leading the group. Chirag was standing behind, feeling shame for the mistakes. I looked at him. He folded both the hands in prayer, but remained mute.

The innocent faces generated warmth of love that could spark even a sleeping heart. Then I had got a pulsating one so, there was no reason of denial.

"Sure, I'll accompany you. Bye the way, where are we going today?" I asked inquisitively.

"Chirag made his way through his friends; came close to me and spoke cheerfully.

"Sir, we are going to The Himalayan Nature Park near Kufri. It's a hunting place for tourists after snowfall. Bye the way, thank you so much, Sir." He ran away whooping with his friends.

It being Sunday, the students could enjoy it in the way they liked. They could decide to watch a movie in Multiplex, organize a get together in school Campus, plan to visit a picnic spot, etc.

Today they all were going to a beautiful picnic spot among hills —Kufri. They all were excited to go out of four walls of the Campus. Only on rare occasions they were allowed to move out so whenever they lucked any such occasion, they felt it as the boon of invisible God.

They all were wearing Jeans; house T-shirt and Jacket. The Wardens were shouting and ordering students to wear caps to avoid cold and fog outside. But the students were moving with fingers in their ears totally unmindful to the orders.

An old man was standing along with Froggy at the gate of Reception Hall observing every activity very minutely. He looked so funny with his mouth open and his eyes bugging wide. His manner was cold and distant. When I passed, he was staring at me with cold eyes. I felt an antipathy to interact him. His face was full of wrinkles and skin so pale that I could see the bone underneath it. His cold gray eyes were full of dirty mischievousness. His long bony hands were instructing the Froggy. I also gave him a cold look and went on.

Actually he had been the owner of the school but I came to know much later on when Rishabh informed me in Bus.

The snow had begun to melt when the bright Sun appeared in the sky illuminating hills and plains all together. When the Buses moved out of Campus, I heard a big uproar from students who breathed the free and fresh air out of Campus.

Inside the Campus, they felt more like chained and fettered, but the moment they had crossed the Campus gate, I could feel the zeal, zest, vigour rejuvenating in them.

They were shouting at their highest pitch in merriment. I felt the caged pigeons coming out of cage and feeling the broad spread sky so they were flying spreading their wings.

They had no fear of Froggy's scolding; the lunch getting cancelled; bevy of questions in the class; and over all the compulsion to speak in English.

They had their own world today and they were all in all in that. They were sitting, dancing standing, leaning on others and were engaged looting the utmost fun they could have in short fast moving time.

Outside the Bus, the roads were neat and clean with the forests of spruce, deodar pine, oak and rhododendron on both the sides. We were having great fun while moving among the sky soaring mountains and rivers gurgling through deep stony gorges, low rolling hills all around. The scene on the way was one of breathtaking beauty. We were passing through the exuberantly green woodlands along the roadside. The journey by Bus gave me an excellent delectation and gratification.

The city was changing its moods at every turn on the road. We saw flowers of all kinds, both wild and cultivated, smiling in each garden at the gate of beautiful Bungalows. There were neat fences at the sides of the road, painted a dainty blue color, and beyond them were the snow capped peaks.

It might have taken almost one and half hour to reach the Destination of Picnic Spot. The place offered panoramic views of the distant Himalayas apart from its beautiful natural surroundings.

Thousands of tourists were enjoying the scenic attractions of the spot. Even though it was winter season, the place was very hot and most haunted by tourists.

The students were not allowed to roam here and there so they were led to the Himalayan Nature Park. It was a wild life sanctuary for animals and birds found in the region. In this park rare varieties of Hangal, Barking Deer, Musk Deer, Brown Bear, rare species of Monal and other pheasants were kept in social groupings. We also saw a vast collection of migratory birds in the Nature Park.

It being little bit foggy, the scenes were a bit dismal in the morning, but when the fog got cleared, we enjoyed the most serene self of Nature in Park. The entire range of the snow clad peaks of Himalaya was one of breathtaking scenes of beauty. Above all the place was *Abode of Peace*.

A few senior students were allowed to enjoy tobogganing and horse riding there, but the junior students were confined to the Park only.

Being unused to the snow, I was shivering though I was wearing my best woolen clothes that were protective enough for any rough weather.

I stopped enjoying in the company of students and sat down in a corner of National Park where the luggage of all the students was kept. I found the place slightly protective from biting puffs of wind. I lay down on the bed sheet at full length, my arms behind my head that I could look down the hill towards the small stream falling from a high hill.

A shadow swept over me. I bounced and felt panic-stricken.

It was a bird of prey looking ferocious. It was flying low over the Park gazing the innocent and meek birds in the cages. I watched it land on the low picket fence that stretched all around the Park. Then it fluttered its blue-black wings and tilted its head. The next moment it made a dive, picked a small bird in its beak and flew in the endless realm of blue-black sky.

Suddenly I saw two strange looking men moving towards me. I had been in the Park for last two hours, but I had not seen them anywhere. They came into view from some unknown corner of the Park.

I felt scared so I moved to the side of senior students.

"What happened sir? Are you all right?" I noticed Chirag feeling worried about me.

"Y-y-yeah, I'm all right." I stuttered.

"Sir, you sit here and enjoy our play. If you need my help any moment, I'll be here at your beck and call." He said and ran away to join his friends.

Those nasty fellows came following me there also. I thought of informing Rishabh regarding my fear, but an idea struck my mind that 'the park is a public place so open to one and all. Anyone can move anywhere'. I stopped looking that side where the unlikable creatures were standing.

I thought 'I should change my place once again. If these horrible figures come chasing me there also, I'll believe that their presence in the garden pose a threat.'

I got up and moved to the cages of the wild birds. The shadows came following from behind. They were about to touch my body that I ran blindly; reached Rishabh gasping.

"Sir, I need your help immediately." I spoke in a breath.

He became active in a jiffy.

"What happened? Are you all right?" He spoke helping me to sit down.

"Can you arrange a vehicle to send me to the Campus? I need to warm myself sitting around bonfire and then covering myself in the heavy quilt." I said shivering with cold.

The extreme cold at night and our playing with powder snow on the roof had affected me badly. Furthermore, the two brutes at my back had enraged my restlessness.

Rishabh called for the Driver who had brought Car for the Lady Teachers.

"Listen, you take Tanmay sir. Drop him in the hostel well. And tell the Cafeteria In-Charge to attend sir." Rishabh ordered the Driver.

"And one thing more, come back in time. Don't swindle anybody on the way." Rishabh warned the Driver.

He took me to the School Car; made me sit comfortably.

I saw the two Bandicoots standing at a distance and gazing at me. I thought they were enjoying my restlessness.

"The car started moving at a fast pace on the narrow road. I felt pretty comfortable when the Driver switched the Heater on. It was pretty warm to have a snooze.

I had hardly fallen in power-nap that I was shaken by big jerk of Car.

I got up with the speed of electricity and saw a luxury-car had hit my car from behind. I was taken aback.

"Slow down the speed and let the other car pass." I suggested the driver and he followed it instantly.

The next moment our car was hit harder than before. I suddenly jumped to the seat beside the driver.

"Drive the car fast; as fast as you can. The man behind us wants to kill us." I shook the driver with both hands.

"Y-ye-yes sir." He stammered and pressed the accelerator.

It was rather hard to drive the Car fast as there were deep valleys on left side and big clefts on the right.

The road was divided by a white line made of paint and it was too narrow for two cars running parallel.

I couldn't get what grievances any person might have against me when I am unknown to this place. I have never hurt anyone or been out of the School Campus still the blood thirsty people behind were after my life in that bloody awful weather.

The body had gone crazed with fear apprehending the crazed killers a few yards back.

The danger was lurking from all the corners. Fear of fall in the deep valley or getting collided head-on was haunting every moment. The turns were so sharp that you couldn't see the vehicle coming from opposite side unless it came quite close.

A small mistake of the driver could lead us to a horrible death. There was no crossing, no police barrier, possibly no help was in view. That was all the more horrifying.

"Our life is in your hands now. Do your best. Apply all your driving skills today and save us." I said boosting up the morale of the driver placing my hand on his shoulder.

He was lost in concentration and driving the Car at the maximum speed possible on that narrow road. We felt a slide at the right back of the Car and apprehended in a second that the moment of death has approached that made my blood freeze.

The demons at the back were pushing our Car in the valley from right side. The speeding Car came parallel to us on the right. We were keeping to the most left. Even a single touch of the enemy car cold could throw our car in the deep valley.

Getting frightened I looked for the Vultures in the sky that will attack on my body soon after death. There was none.

Now I looked at the driver and then at the Car running parallel to us. The sight pulverized me. The same Bandicoots were laughing at me. Their activities were the warnings of impending danger.

I knew that the inevitable had come imminent. I closed my eyes; felt sorry for my family members; opened the eyes and felt my hackles rise.

"Push their car to the right before they push ours. Let them collide with the Cars from opposite side or feel the friction of the cliff.

The driver gave a powerful hit in the car. The first time I felt their car bobbled and the fear on their faces.

The Driver gave another hit to them before they could manage, and left their imbalanced Car to collide with another fast pacing Car from the front. Only we could see the head on Car because of a very sharp turn to the right side.

We heard a loud collision at the back. The car had just drifted off the road and slid down the mountain hurling to the left. The other car had completely flipped over. Suddenly the world stopped moving. The rollover caused traffic tie-up.

He pulled me back from the brink. A sharp cry left my lips, a cry that no one seemed to hear. My driver had pressed the accelerator to the floor of the Car and we had reached too ahead to stick in traffic Jam.

We dared not to see or even enquire of the accident behind and ran to our Campus with the speed of storm.

Behind the endless trees, I saw a small creek that followed the road. Sunlight sparkled on its frozen surface.

The most weird and unexpected mishap on the road had shaken me to the roots. The car had reached the School Campus. The guard at the gate had built a fire to keep chill out of his room. I, therefore, requested the driver to drop me at the gate. I reached the guard shivering all over with cold and fear.

The guard left his chair for me and sat on his heels. I sat in his chair, facing the crackling fire, my chin resting on my hands. The irregular beatings of my heart responded to the faint murmur of the fire and the sound of dropping of a cinder from the bars.

When the fire had died down on the surface, he poked at it with a long stick and again there were sparks rising from inside. Meanwhile, the driver reached with a tumbler of tea in his hands for me.

"Sir, the Car is damaged. The police on the road may stop me and look into the cause. Allow me to take another car.

"Do you have the key?" I asked without giving my ear to his words.

"Yes, the keys are with the Security-in-Charge. If you say him once, he'll give me." he suggested politely.

"Go and take the keys. I'll give him a call." I said.

The Driver took a turn to go.

"Wait! Listen! Don't drive the car fast!" I suggested.

He went nodding.

The sun had gone high in the sky above the hills, and playing hide and seeks with the clouds. But the shiver in breeze was tingling to the nerves and freezing the bones. The fire had died out deadening the zeal and vigour of the heart. The wet paths, shaking trees in the garden, frightening figures moving around and the crushed flowers in my room led me think, "I had come to a wrong station."

CHAPTER EIGHTEEN

Death Knocks at the Door

I had hurt too much to sleep. When I woke up, it hurt me more so I tried to go back to sleep. There was a physical ache, a gnawing. My body tried vainly to beat down and might have if the pain in my mind wasn't even worse. Processions of thoughts hammered at me; gouged and scraped until the brain was wild thing seeking some kind of release. But there wasn't any release. There was fire all around me, the tongues of it licking closer, needling the skin. The brain screamed for me to awaken, but if did, I knew the other things…the thoughts, would be a more searing pain so I fought until the mind conquered and I felt the awakening coming on.

I thought I heard voices and one was Aanya's. She kept calling to me and I couldn't answer back. She was in some trouble. She was screaming for me. Somebody was hurting her and I mouthed silent curses while I fought invisible bonds that held me tied to the bed. She was screaming. Her voice tortured and I was helpless. I strained and kicked and fought but the ropes held until I was breathless and I had to lie there and listen to her die.

I opened my eyes and looked into the darkness, knowing it was only a dream. My breathing was harsh. I wiped the sleep from my eyes and the beads of sweat from my face.

In broad daylight the events of the night before seemed like a bad dream. The breaths were still fast. I heard a big knock and heavy hustle and bustle in the corridor. On opening the door, I saw Aanya with doom on her face indicating the impending danger.

Her jumbled words were so weird and confusing that I failed to form meaningful sentences. I made her sit comfortably in my room asked her what happened.

She narrated the horror of the day.

"Sir, you must have seen the owner of the school?" she asked quickly and unexpectedly.

"Yeah, I saw him today only. He is rather old. Is there anything serious about him?" I asked getting anxious.

"Actually, he was returning from the city in his car. The driver was driving the car. On a sharp turn, the car collided head on with a speeding car. The collision was so furious that his car slid in the deep valley." She screamed through tears.

She gasped for breath; stared at my blank expressions; realized the trauma inside me and kept looking at me for my reaction.

"Yeah, what happened further?" I uttered out of pity and surprise.

The words started out of her. They came slow at first, and then turned into a boiling current that was taking in the whole picture.

"The dead body has been found with two other persons. One is driver and the other one has been reported to be a notorious thug. The police are investigating the case." She informed hurriedly.

I felt nerve wracking at her words though I was never of a nervous disposition. An uneasy silence had fallen among us and we rode for a time without saying a word. There were tears in the corners of her eyes, little drops of crystal that swelled and I took a step closer to her.

"Hey, why are you in such a shock-horror state?" I broke silence and asked cupping her face in my hands.

"He was the love of my life here in the Campus. He never let me feel that I am away from my family members. He cared for me more than I realized.... The school will remain closed tomorrow. Resident teachers have to be a part of the Puja Ceremony tomorrow." She spoke further.

Her words sent something racing up my back. I arranged her jumbled words.

"How could everything go so disastrously wrong?" I thought.

"Puja Ceremony? What's that?" I nerved myself to ask her out.

"It's a ceremony that is performed every year in the Campus in the month of December. It's ritual to secure our Campus from some unknown dangers." She spoke hurriedly.

"But why? Is there any specific cause behind all this?" I asked inquisitively.

"I don't have any more knowledge about this matter. Nobody is allowed to poke his nose in this issue.... Don't be so inquisitive. It's none of our business! Furthermore, if we are not careful, we could finish up seriously ill." She finished speaking.

Glum looks on her face reflected piled agony caused by the owner's tragic death while the tug of war inside me shook the Earth beneath my feet. I was unable to find my voice and the way.

She got up in the same agonized state and left the room. I was paralyzed to hold her back. The tumult of the day's ferocious mishap was so heavy on me that the surge of fear caused my heart to gallop.

I was left thinking all alone in my room. Today's events were stamped on my brain too clearly and burningly, like the brand of a red-hot iron.

I was going mad through the weary days and restless nights. My hot eyeballs had not a tear to shed, and even to weep was a luxury denied me.

The plastic and undisciplined mind was rushing in the gloomy corners of disbelief and misbelieves. Some impish and malignant faces were gibbering at me from the darkling corners of the room. I suddenly had so many questions running through my mind: Was he the owner of the school chasing my car? Why did he send those bandicoots in the garden? What personal grievances had he against me? Why did he want to throw my car in the deep valley? What profit he might have reaped after my death?

"It's all so weird" I thought.

All of these were sixty-four thousand dollars questions for me and to seek their answers was all the more important. A burning sensation began to grow in my chest. I, therefore, climbed on my bed and comforted my body.

Had the veil of the future been lifted for one instant! But that veil is impenetrable to our gaze.

I shivered at the thought.

"I'll never sleep again, I thought. Not as long as I have to live here." I decided and crept back to bed.

The blight and the sorrow of the moment sent chill to the spine. I pulled my quilt up to my chin. I kept staring the blue ocean and the painted ship on the wallpaper by my head.

Every time I closed my eyes, I saw a shapeless figure hovering over me. I guess I finally dozed off after midnight.

CHAPTER NINETEEN

The Doom Approaches

When I opened my eyes, light screamed in through my window. It was Christmas Day, the next morning after the nasty accident among the hills. The disagreeable sensation still prevailed in my heart. I rubbed the sleep from my eyes.

It being winter, the weather was too cold. It was a dark, moist Yule —not a snowy one, though snow brooded overhead in the darkling clouds.

The bygone ill happenings in the Campus were like a nightmare. I felt as if I had listened to a weird a legend, which my grandfather used to tell exceedingly well. He narrated stories always relating to demonology and witchcraft, for my entertainment.

It was Christmas, the season for such tales; and my room, with its dusky walls and pictures, and vaulted roof, drinking up the daylight so greedily, seemed just fitted to give effect to such legendary lore.

The huge logs crackled and burned with glowing warmth at the Reception building; the blood-red glare of the Yule log flashed on the faces of the listeners and narrator, on the portraits, and the holly wreathed about their frames, and the upright old saintly figure, in his antiquated dress and trinkets, like one of the originals of the pictures, stepped from the canvas to join the congregation. It threw a shimmering luster of an ominously ruddy hue upon the oaken panels.

Though the teachers and students wished "Merry Christmas" to each other, the gaiety of the occasion and the glow of the faces were missing. Everyone was busy contributing to the grand *Puja Ceremony*.

The Brahmins, Fakirs, Saints, Quacks, Mendicants and all sorts of people could be seen moving in the Campus.

The students were confined to the hostel only. They were allowed to move out to the Cafeteria only in the supervision of the Wardens.

The security at the gate was high. The strictness in the hostel rose. No student could be seen out of the dormitory. They were not allowed to move in the Corridor even. Even the birds were hovering and flying away from the Campus. The dogs were paralyzed and sitting coiled in the corners.

The scenario was all amazing and shocking. I had never seen that much silence in the hostel ever before.

The Sun was also playing hide and seek behind the hills and under a heavy cover of fog and mist.

The Nature was proclaiming the befalling danger outdoors. The blowing storm was making heavy strokes on face and humming not to go forth.

The foul, mysterious and gloomy looks of the Quacks and Sorcerers was sending a ferocious stir to the bones. The blood in veins was trying to maintain the normal speed against the freezing chill.

Reception Hall was the most hunting place of the day. All mysterious kind of people from all religions had collected there performing certain rituals. Some faces were so horrible that they seemed pally with Satan or practicing black magic.

Some religious, grave old persons could be seen sprinkling Holy Water in the Campus as a Christmas day ritual. The air floating in the Campus had a purified fragrance of incenses used by Holy Saints in the ritual.

The smoke could be seen coming out of the Reception Hall. A large Fire Sacrifice was lit to purify the Campus air. It was also organized to send peace and comfort to the soul of the old owner who died miserably in an accident.

The gathered clouds in the sky warned against imminent downpour. The winds howling sent a chilling horror down to the spine. I turned down the idea of moving out of the room in such odd and nasty weather.

CHAPTER TWENTY

A Shortcut to Hell

There had been a violent thunderstorm earlier, the sky had cleared afternoon, now it was raining again, a hard rain with thunder and wind that tore the gorgeous leaves from the thick woods.

The Campus had become a hotbed of unknown rituals. It gave me an itch along the spine, excited dread, and stimulated curiosity.

Finally I got bored with myself and my predicaments. Though winter did not suit my veins, I decided to go forth. I opened the door to a cold breeze and heavy rain.

Aanya came from behind silently on rubber soles and touched my spine; I jumped and frowned.

"Take it easy. I always act like a total jerk." she said passing a smile.

"Every touch in the Campus is scary; everyman doubtful; and every breeze foul with the nasty happenings." I spoke in frustration. "By the way, why is there such a big gathering of religious persons?" I asked.

"Oh, never mind. You just get in. It's too cold here. You'll catch cold easily." She spoke pushing me inside my room.

"Every time, you are worried for all this nonsense. Never thinks of me. You…." I stopped her mouth with a kiss.

I parted my lips and made her sit on the settee comfortably; gave her a shawl to cover herself.

My face had a worried look that Aanya didn't fail to read. She made me sit comfortably by her side.

"Dear! Why do you look so burdened, nervous and anxious? Give a tongue to your anxieties and let your heart feel light.

I felt a bit relaxed but the anxiety in was so powerful to find suitable words.

"Honey, there is now a stir and bustle in me going all time. The notion of an unseen presence of the shadow doesn't let me rest. My nerves are shaken by the ghastly lore prevailing here. I feel myself a weak, superstitious creature, unable to pass a night even in my room." I spoke looking into her eyes.

"Whatever nasty we come across at night, we let the impression die out before sunrise. When the bright sun shines on the frosted boughs, and the rime on the grass, we become resilient. How long it will last, we have no idea. Every time we cherish the childish hope of being redeemed by God. Nonsense! If we don't initiate to discover the cause and reveal the mystery, who the heck is going to sort it out?" I expressed my anxiety placing my hands gently on her shoulder to emphasize my words.

"We don't need having fits, screaming and waking in the middle of the night. We don't have to wait for—what will happen ere another day dawn? But we have to make an end of this Phantom tale. I feel ashamed to speak of such matters before these hard-headed, unimaginative men, who had no sympathy with people abroad. I just don't like to gossip about the folks I work for. Hillbilly says that this place is a shortcut to hell." I grumbled my words on her.

Suddenly I felt her body trembling. Her sudden movement startled me. I shrank back, thinking she planned to hurt me....

"How are we concerned with the ill happenings here? Why should we risk our lives to explore the mystery?" She asked getting restless.

"Sometimes you do things you're afraid of because you're more afraid of how you'll turn out if you don't." I took a pause; called up a smile and an air of mirth.

"There's no reason to panic now. We are very near to solve this puzzle. What we need is to work united." I consoled her.

Chirag and his group will also assist us. I have informed them to join us at 11 o'clock. Now you go and take rest. I'll wake you up in the nick of time.

CHAPTER TWENTY ONE

Horror of the Horrors
(*Things that go bump in the night*)

The rain had stopped for a while, but there were still little flashes of lightening, faint rumbles of thunder. On that night everyone was afraid to go out.

The mind was travelling with the rotating hand of the clock on the wall. The soft ticking of the clock was hammering in the eyes.

At quarter past 11, I walked to the hostel to look in on Chirag, who was sleeping at the edge of the bed, one foot almost touching the floor. I moved him and pulled the covers up shaking him. He responded and got engaged in waking up his companions silently.

Then I turned to Aanya's room. The door was not latched from within. I opened it very softly to avoid banging.

She was lying on the antique-white satin coverlet of her mahogany bed, her head resting on the pillows, her luminous brown eyes wide and shining with desire. The soft white batiste of her long skirt rode high on her shapely thighs. A small pillow lay beneath the top blanket, and it was brand new. A teddy bear waited beside the new pillow that seemed smiling at me.

My mouth reached hers on the bed then, finally. And she parted her lips and welcomed me. Outside the window was the soft glow of the moonlight and across the room the candle guttered and went out.

The heart thought otherwise, but the mind prevented so I shook her right hand and indicated to join in my room.

Everyone had collected. We were five in number. The silence on the faces of everyone was murderous and gave a goose pimple yet no one felt scared to investigate. The dark serious eyes of the Daredevils were burning into mine. I was well aware of the risk involved in the dare. The students loved challenges so they were straining at the leash to explore. We took our flashlight; assigned certain codes and set out on our mission to investigate the source of the phantom story.

The comets were flashing across the sky and proclaiming the coming calamity. There was deathly hush all around the hostel. Aanya shuddered in the night wind, hugging herself. She had put on a black jacket and Jeans. The lights were flashing so we had to take care at every step. She was walking holding my hands and the Daredevils behind. We were spooked by the strange noises and lights in Reception Hall. Before we could give a second thought, we heard a loud rumbling of thunder. The hearts sank.

The tall, old-fashioned-looking streetlamps cast circles of blue-white light along the street. The thunder growled menacingly and the trees, trembling ghostlike in heavy gusts of wind, rustled over the sidewalk, as we stepped beneath them.

A few yards away we heard a movement under the trees in the Garden. We ducked back out of the light, behind a wide tree trunk. A strange feeling of dread swept over us. I took a shawl from Chirag and crept out from behind the tree and hurried away along the wall of the Sports Ground hiding myself from the flash lights to make sure if it was danger free.

I moved stealthily like a true spy taking care of the flashing lights. The leaves of the trees were creating a confused sound to have a clear feel of the pulse of the Danger lurking.

I listened secretly the feminine whispers that were coming out of shrubs as black as the sky. A chill ran down all my body. I was dumb silent; quite conscious to all sides and shivering all over. I froze in the same shapeless state so the voices could not figure out that someone is eavesdropping from the other side of the shrubs.

I was standing in such an uncomfortable state that it sent scary messages to my heart. If the Daredevils or Aanya had seen me standing in slanting posture and the hands in flying mode, they would have definitely felt scared and run away proclaiming our presence out of the Hostel.

In a couple of seconds, something moving through the trees caught my eyes. I saw a strange male figure appearing from nowhere among the shrubs and going towards the building under construction at this hour.

Every breeze was spooky in the campus and every sound blood-curdling. Aanya hiding at a distance was also looking like a shadow and my heart was frightened to think of her activities.

"What on earth I'm doing here when my own shadow seems scary." I muttered under my breath and ducked behind the shrubs.

I ducked low when Hillbilly passed by the side of the shrubs in his intoxication. Earlier he never looked on his either side and kept moving talking to himself, but today he was extra conscious. He was looking in all the directions though he was well aware that no one was allowed to move out of rooms that night.

When Hillbilly had completely vanished in the shadow, the Voices on the other side of the shrubs seemed lengthening their shadows and chasing Hillbilly. I stood up slowly and raised myself on tiptoes to see over the shrubs. I waited for my eyes to adjust in the dark. Taking a deep breath, I stepped out from behind the shrubs; rushed back to the Daredevils and asked them to follow us from a distance.

The moving familiar shadows of the Daredevils and others frightened me, reminded me of the menacing Dark Figure that had caused so many damages in the Campus.

In the thick woods, we were huddled together, keeping close to the school boundary and following the feminine shadows closely. Aanya recognized the voices and hushed a whisper "These female devils are Meghana and her friends."

I felt relaxed to think that they were human figures and not shadows. But at the same time it felt quite weird to see the girls out of the hostel at night and that too when it was abandoned.

Meanwhile Aanya nudged me and whispered indicating her finger. Before she could vibrate her lips, I hushed her voice with my right palm.

We saw the Hillbilly entering the Building under construction and the girls chasing him after. A shiver of fear ran down my back.

No, please! I wanted to cry.

Don't go in the Building! Don't go in there!

But it was too late. I shuddered at the thought how the girls could be so daring or stupid to enter a building at this dark hour when they didn't know whether humans live there or spirits.

Don't they realize how much trouble they could get into?

By the way, I should run to help them. By the time, Chirag and his friends had reached us and saw the feminine figures disappearing in the building. I felt my muscles tighten in dread. I could tell they were as scared as I was.

"Be alert and vigilant. We have to save them from unknown danger." I murmured stupidly in the dead of night.

Aanya stuck close by my side.

Then without thinking about the consequences, without even realizing the lurking danger, we were running too. In a few seconds we were at the construction building, breathing hard.

We saw a few flashes of torches on the first floor so we hid behind the stairs on the ground floor.

We felt the darkness circle wrapped around us tightly. The girls were running here and there frenziedly or in panic. They had been searching for Hillbilly who had been vanished from their sight in the dark.

Then we heard a shrill creaking coming from the building. It sounded much like an old door swinging open and shut. A chill of fear shot down my back.

We cautiously made our way toward the sound. To our surprise, we noticed a small window on the ground floor, swinging back and forth, making the shrill creaking noise.

Another moment we heard a sound near the extreme right wall of the building. I asked Chirag to hold the lead and I rushed out. I was shocked to see Hillbilly going back. The feeling of dread suddenly became over-powering. My knees trembled and I felt cold all over.

"He might have jumped from the wall seeing the girls." I whispered under my breath.

I was in a quandary—should I catch the Hillbilly alone or I should prefer the safety of Aanya and the students inside the building in the grip of dark. I tried to shout, but the voice was muffled in its heavy darkness. The entire body tightened with fear.

Before I could decide anything, I heard screams in terror from inside the building. I rushed in. Chirag had already taken the charge and was on the flight of stairs. The other Daredevils were with Aanya on the foot stair rushing to the danger end. We saw the girls running madly as if they had encountered any shadow. But before we could catch them, they went downstairs from the other end of the building. There was pitch darkness so we could not run after the girls. If we had flashed our light, they would have felt more scared and would have jumped directly from the first floor in panic consequently leading to a great danger.

Breathing hard, we began to creep toward the cries in Darkness. Chirag now flashed the light and showed us the way to go downstairs.

"Sir, you take Ma'am from here safely and wait for us at the Gate or go and inform the lady warden about the girls. We would stay here and like to know the reason why Meghana and her friends felt appalled."

Aanya was horrified; her face was changing expressions and her ruby eyes were burnt like fire so I preferred going to Girls' hostel and let her take rest.

I asked Chirag to take care of himself and his friends.

"I'll be back in few seconds. Don't stay here inside the building much longer. It's biting cold. We don't have to sacrifice our lives." I muttered and moved supporting Aanya who was half conscious only.

The girls' Hostel was not far away so I moved in that direction. Another squeamish sight dazzled my eyes. I saw the girls entering the hostel boundary not from the main gate but with the support of a ladder that they had placed against the wall near the balcony of the first floor.

I had reached the main gate of the Girls Hostel and was about to coax the bell. I had no fear while disturbing the Senior Girls Warden at night as Aanya was with me. She was also the In-charge of the hostel in her absence.

I had hardly touched the door bell switch when I heard the girls on the first floor screaming again. I pulled my hand back; left Aanya there at the gate and ran to the ladder that was still propped against the back wall.

The girls had seen a shadow moving on the first floor. When they saw me, they screamed all the more considering me a ghost.

I didn't waste my time and rushed close to them. When they recognized me under the light in corridor, they stopped screaming and hugged me from all sides. I stood aghast at the sight of so much blood in their hands. They had forgotten their blood stained hands so their hug had wiped all the blood on my black Shawl. When they spoke, their words dismayed me.

"Sir, the Water-Cooler is pouring blood in place of water." The fear had made their tongue slow and voice hesitant.

I stared in horror and disbelief, struggling to breathe. Their voices were as dry as dead leaves. I couldn't make out anything so I pushed them to go in their rooms first. I thought to go down and enter from the main gate with Aanya and then enquire into the case so I turned to the Balcony.

I was on the top most stair of the ladder that I heard the Daredevils shouting at the top of their lungs. Their sneakers thudded against the pavement of the sidewalk. A terrible thought flashed through my mind. A burst of frigid air encircled my body. I wanted to reply but my voice caught in my throat. The heart beat reached very near to heart attack so I jumped from there. The fall took my breaths away, but luckily I landed on my both legs. I balanced myself. The knees were throbbing with pain and heart was thudding loudly still I rushed blindly for the safety of Aanya. I could hear the muffled voices inside and the scrape of sneakers on the pavement. The guards in the campus had become alert. They could be seen rushing to our side.

I stared in horror. Aanya was safe standing at the gate.

I took a deep breath and gazed around the heavy blackness.

"Aanya, are you okay?" I asked. My voice came out tiny and shrill.

Chirag reached us faster than Guards. His long hair was matted against his forehead from sweat. Their faces wore frightened expressions and the light from the street lamp made their faces look pale. Chirag was a bit spooked while narrating the horror he had come across.

"Sir, there is a lady in yellow dress hanging in one of the rooms in the building. All the four walls are blood stained. The most surprising is that there is no spot of blood on her dress." He finished hurriedly.

My legs were shaking so hard, I could barely stand. I found myself entangled in the labyrinth of horrors. The whole Campus—Academic Blocks, Hostel Buildings, Reception Hall, the Building under Construction and the Woods—seemed haunted.

The guards had reached there, but didn't say anything to the students as they noticed me and Aanya with the students. But the story they had heard was enough to make them run to the side of the building.

I struggled to catch my breath. The intimidating happening all around had unnerved my all senses. We had failed to discover the source and cause of paranormal events. The hair all over the body had stood on its ends. We had no other option but to enter the Reception Hall and ask the religious persons if there was any end to this hair-raising terror so we blindly rushed to be a part of the happenings.

CHAPTER TWENTY TWO

Necromancers Around Sacred Wood

It was quarter to 12 at night. My mind was spinning in confusion, feeling dazed and terrified. I reached the Reception Hall leaving Aanya and the Daredevils hidden behind nearby. My eyes opened wide with surprise when I viewed a sight that sensed of impending doom. The sight was so unreal that I could hardly believe what was going on. The Hall was full of pious smoke that was rising from the Fire Sacrifice. Occult practitioners—the Priests, Mendicants, Quakers, Exorcists—all were busy chanting the mantras and offering sacred materials in fire to produce some black magic. Their practice seemed invoking or calming the rage of the Supernatural Powers, entities, spirits, and the like which inhabited the realms of School.

There was a strange look on the dark broad faces of the occultists and Sorcerers that gave the look that these Powers—Earthly Wizard, Witches, Demons, Spirits or Ghosts were in their control. When the Puja Ceremony would get over, they believed to gain control over Paranormal Powers, or the Sorcery would willingly submit to their demands.

I also noticed Froggy, white-haired and wearing glasses, sitting around the fire with a handkerchief on his head. He looked haggard and drawn. He felt bewildered to notice me at the gate. There was hustle and bustle among the occultists. Their eyes gave me a stern look. Froggy got up; beckoned everyone to continue and stepped towards me.

He looked depressed and afraid. His expression was one such frozen bleakness that it made me shiver. I had never seen such a cold look in anyone's eyes before. When I enquired into, there was a look like death warmed up in his eyes for an instant that he tried to hide from me. He was looking at me now, his eyes glittering almost feverishly, high color burning over his cheekbones almost as though he had a fever. He looked ill and in a state of trauma. I realized worriedly, his skin beneath that hectic flush an unhealthy grayish color.

I also stepped towards him automatically, stopping in shock when he raised his hands as though to rebuff me.

"Tanmay," He told me harshly, "you must not have come out of your room at this hour. There is a great danger lurking in the dark here. We are having a problem with the Christmas night. You just don't ask any question right now. I'll satisfy all your queries in day light. Let me complete the Puja. You just retire to your room and have rest, being unmindful to all this."

Froggy's suggestion sent a sudden rush of fear down my spine. He was quite abrupt with me almost to the point of dislike.

I heard a roar and panic in the Hall and the same time a loud shriek in Horror at the Gate of the Hall. In a jiffy, I recognized that it was Aanya's voice. Before I could decide my course of action, the Daredevils let out another piercing shriek.

"Tanmay Sir!"

I ran to their side in a frenzy of atavistic fear. My heart thumped up hard, I thought it might burst out of my chest. The violent storm with thunder and lightning dazzled my eyes and gave a halt. I saw Aanya rushing towards the thick Garden and the Daredevils transfixed with shock. I knew that I had to confront my fears so I made a direct flight to catch Aanya who seemed possessed.

Froggy ran to stop and save me, but fell down. He saw the lightning flare on the doomed skylight directly overhead, and a lot of sparklers. Injury only added to his terror.

He struggled to his feet. He was tipsy, couldn't stand without hanging on to something. When he tried to take a step his feet got tangled. The free-fall of sparklers continued. He saw something rise up between him and the emergency lights, blotting them out. He tried to scream and could only gargle a sob.

CHAPTER TWENTY THREE

The Love of My Life

My blood grew chill and curdled; the flesh crept; the heart beat irregularly. I gave a hard and blind chase towards the garden. The howling wind sounded like the wailing of lost souls.

The Moon had appeared in the Sky from nowhere. At few places the leaves were so thick they nearly blocked the moonlight. I was standing among the shaking trees but there wasn't a soul in sight. I ran to the last end of the Garden and saw a figure slid out from behind a tree. I gasped and stopped walking as if paralyzed with fear.

At first I thought it was just the shadow cast by the wide trunk. But then, as my eyes adjusted to the shade, the figure became clear. It was coming to closer and closer. I suddenly gripped with a cold feeling. I could see her properly. She was not a shadow, but a ravishing beauty like a fairy hardly fifteen years.

She stood in a deep blue puddle of shadow. Dressed in white, she was a tall, slender and shapely girl with long straight strawberry blonde hair, peaches and cream complexion and a pair of smoldering brown eyes that set my heart alight.

I felt a cold shiver of fear roll down my body.

"Is she Aanya? Aanya can never play horror especially when the lives are at stake." I looked for her in all the darks. I felt as if a hundred eyes were stalking me through the trees.

"Who is she then?" I wondered, "Why is she dressed like that?"

"Why is she standing so still, keeping in the shadows, staring back at me from the dark shade?"

"Is she trying to scare me?"

My heart fluttering in my chest, I took a step back.

"Is there really someone there? A figure dressed in white?"

"Or am I seeing shadows cast by the trees?"

I wasn't sure until I heard the whisper.

"Sarthak.... Sarthak...."

The whisper was as dry as the brush of tree leaves, and nearly as soft.

"Sarthak...Sarthak...."

I got the fright of my life when I reminded of the horrible night when I heard these words in the darkness of my room.

A slender white shadow was motioning to me with arms as bony as twigs, and whispering to me—such a dry, inhuman whisper.

I argued with myself. An optical illusion doesn't call my name.

I spun around and struggled to run. My legs felt weak. My knees forbade bending.

The sweet jingling of her anklets intoxicated my ears. Her sudden movement startled me. I shrank back, thinking she planned to hurt me. The white enshrouded figure that had whispered an unfamiliar name was so close to me that I could touch her. She looked into my eyes and hypnotized.

The enchantress enthralled me and took me to a small platform in the garden; made me sit there. She perched herself uncomfortably on the edge and grew fondly affectionate to me. She spoke in a language which was very loving, and assured me not to fear from her.

"I'm Anushka, your forbidden love."

She released the painful breath she had been holding.

CHAPTER TWENTY FOUR

An Amiable Touch of Reality

It was twenty five years before when we were the students of Class 10 here in the same school. I was the daughter of the Owner of the school who died in accident recently. You got admission the same year in 10th. It was the month of August quite chilly weather. I was in class when you walked in. You were handsome, smart, tall, attractive, black hair—all-round nice personality—Mr. Perfect in the class. All girls felt infatuated with you but me.

And then, what could have been more amazing and nervously coincidental at the same time, the teacher asked you to sit next to me.

Before your arrival in the school, I was considered the topper in the class. I was very arrogant and overbearing. Moreover I was the daughter of the Owner so I could never tolerate anyone better in Academics than me in class. Whenever the teacher asked any question in the class, you had a prompt answer. It was not like I didn't know the answer but my mind was obsessed with jealousy so it never responded quickly. Every time I was burning in the fire of envy.

The next week there was a debate competition organized in our school. Being jealous, I labored too hard just to defeat you before all. I was least bothered about my success but more concerned about your defeat.

When the actual hour reached, I did my best and when you expressed your points, I put fingers in the both the ears. I was dead sure that I would be declared the winner. But the fate had set against me. The Judges liked your points more. They invited you to the stage. When you were honored on the stage, you took the mike and requested the Jury to receive the trophy from the hands of the last year's winner. *That was me.* The tears of gloom got converted into the flicker of smile. I rushed to the platform and stood by the side of my father.

When the trophy was brought to the stage, I felt as the happiest soul upon the Earth. By the time I had forgotten the envy and my defeat. I put down my antagonism to attraction. I felt more honorable while holding the Trophy than if I had won and received the trophy.

When I raised my hands to offer the Trophy to you, you looked like the angel descended for me and I felt my search for soul mate over. I had always dreamt of finding my one lifelong friend, my partner, my soul mate who would be there for me in my time of need and who could delight, thrill and entertain me in a unique way. In addition to conversation on a deep level and an understanding of my little idiosyncrasies and irritations that in turn strengthened our bond and sincere connection with each other. I was joyous for our burgeoning friendship.

I thought as if you were sent by some mysterious force to be in the same place at the same time. Someone had been picking up on my subconscious messages into the universe to find my lifelong friend and soul mate.

I looked at you and said softly, "since we've now made our peace with one another, we should perhaps seal it in the time honored way" and you gave a nod of approval.

The very moment I felt endorsing our peace treaty with the seal of a deep kiss on your rosy lips, but the presence of my father stopped me.

That day in the evening sports, we had so much fun that seemed to go on forever. We played, we hugged, we kissed, we spoke, we laughed, but most of all—we knew....

When I asked you, "Why did you receive the Trophy from my hands?"

You were so silent, serene and spoke with great affection, "Anushka, you had won the competition many times and received the honor publicly. Only you could understand the real importance of getting Trophy. Your father, the teachers and your friends had always seen the trophy in your hands on the stage. Today also they wanted to see the Trophy in your hands first. I could never break the hearts of so many and above all yours. When the Trophy was brought and you held it in both of your hands, the hearts of all present felt overjoyed. That was true spirit of competition, winning and appreciation."

Your response made me shiver and felt Goosebumps. Your voice was warm and low, sending shivers of delight racing up and down my spine. I blushed scarlet at the thought. I felt tingly all over. My stomach flipped flopped and I had butterflies in it. I felt warm and fuzzy. I felt like crying when I bade you goodbye.

Though you had departed, your words along with your sweet face kept coaxing my heart all the night. I felt that you keep sleeping by the silent crystalline streams in the darkness of my dreams and all of my fourteen years I never knew you were the dream I would see coming true. I was the one who looked so hard, I could not see, and then I could never live without seeing you even for a day. I lived like a wild and lonely soul, lost in a dream beyond control. You were the one who brought me home. I knew 'Love comes swiftly, and it's easy and perfectly acceptable to become lost in love.' My heart started to thump unevenly, tiny frissons of excitement curling my nerve-endings.

Then our bond just grew and grew and continued to get stronger day by day. You were loving, generous, adorable and most of all, my best friend!

We used to walk through the little woods every day, just enjoying the trees and birds and the shared solitude. You brought me a flower the next day.

You nodded with a very shy smile. I smiled back and nodded. You took both my hands in yours and pressed them to your heart. No words were necessary.

It often felt like I had known you forever. The days became crisp and the leaves began to change, a vivid color displayed amidst the evergreens. I felt feelings building for you. I started looking forward to spending the rest of my life with you. And then one day, I looked up at you as you slipped your fingers between mine and I knew you were the one that I loved.

I would just look at you and wanted to put my arm around you, hold your hand and kiss you passionately. We would sit here for hours in front of this flower plant much like this one, silent together; similar in temperament, not needing to speak, our souls whispered intimately. I subdued an aching impulse to reach out and touch you, to place my lips to your warm brown skin and breathe in the vital male scent of yours.

You became a part of me and my heart always went out to you. Behind your graciously good looks was faith, kindness, intelligence, and honesty and I wouldn't trade the world for you.

I was a sophomore in school and going to celebrate my 15th Birthday. I had ambitions and dreams so I had never thought that I would be the girl to fall in love like that. Once you asked me to marry you. Tears of joy ran immediately in my eyes and I said "yes". I wanted to yell at the top of my lungs from the rooftop, "I love you and I'll wait for you till eternity." You comforted me and soothed me by shrouding me in the warmth of your embrace and advised "Love is always patient and kind. First we should build our careers and then live a blissful married life."

I had never been happier in my life than when I was with you. The days rolled smoothly; we used to watch the sunset lying together on the grass in the garden. I didn't want the days to end and neither did you.

CHAPTER TWENTY FIVE

The Ways of Love don't Run Smooth

The bliss we felt was interrupted by the Lady Warden Ms. Vidhya who was very pally with my father. She threatened me in the hostel to inform my parents if I continued my friendship with you. I didn't care for anyone but you, so the issue got serious and my father was informed about all this.

He came and took me home; advised me; threatened me; warned me to get away from you. I accepted frankly "I can live without breaths for a couple of seconds, but not without Sarthak." He felt offended; slapped me and threatened me against your life and career.

I didn't surrender. I was ready to die with you; leave the Campus and my parents for you. My father knew it very well so he never stopped me interacting with you, but he didn't permit our love.

Once when the Hostlers went for outing at Kufri, we were quite happy talking and playing with each other. The innocent birds in the cages of the National Park were so good to look at. The whole world had come concise in your arms only. I didn't want to come back to hostel, but to run away in the realms of romance and the soaring heights of the beautiful sky like a dove. The life seemed to present the rainbow of happiness with both hands. A single sight of yours fetched more happiness than the accumulated wealth of the whole world. Life had no demands but your presence, your company, your love, your words and above all your care.

The shining snow-capped in the lap of Nature resembled the beautiful figures of the white suit I was wearing. You sat down against me and composed a love song in my name. The song had all the rosy colors of love between us. The world looked fresh and new with no malice around. The warmth of love in eyes had removed the dirt of evils.

I had your image in waking or sleeping eyes. The world had become a small nest of two singing birds that were happy to share the care of their lives.

The beautiful surroundings seemed inviting and we rushed to have a view of the deep valley from the edge the low picket fence that stretched all around the Park.

In a flash two bandicoots came from nowhere and disturbed our peaceful world. They seemed having some grievances with our love.

They pushed you from that hill in the deep Valley. I gave a cry of anguish and rushed to your side. The sight was so shocking that the next moment I fell down unconscious.

She wiped the tears rolling down her eyes, comforted her excited emotions and then resumed.

When I came to my senses, I was in Hospital surrounded by my parents. I enquired about you. I was reported that you were well. Only slight injuries were there so your parents came and took you home. I was not allowed to go to school for many days.

Once I was playing on the Terrace of my house, I saw that bandicoot that pushed you from the height was talking to my father. My suspicion deepened and tension heightened.

I wanted to go to hostel as quickly as possible. I pretended that I was all right and ready to begin my study. I was sent to school in a couple of days.

In class, hostel or school no one used to interact with me. I was isolated and felt freaked. Even my friends were not ready to tell anything about you.

I reminded of Niharika in junior hostel. You loved her as your sister. She had also tied *Rakhi* on your hand when you had not gone to your home after admission.

I being the daughter of the Owner was always under the watch of the teachers and warden. The Guards were very strict with me; my sports in the evening were cancelled. I was confined to hostel dormitory after school. One night when the lights were off, I got up stealthily and went to Niharika's room. She was sleeping. I woke her up. When she saw me, she felt shaken then she put her hands around my waist and started sobbing.

I took her out in Wash Room. There she informed me weeping.

"Sarthak Bhaiya died falling from the hill. His dead body was found the next day of outing." She also told me that "There is a rumor among the students in the school that your father sent those persons who pushed Sarthak Bhaiya."

I didn't weep; I didn't feel puzzled; I didn't approach police to give evidences against my father. I only wanted to be with you either in life or in death. Death held no terror for me as the living creatures.

The warden had woken up and was searching for me. She caught me moving in the Corridor so shouted a lot. I said nothing and went to my bed.

I didn't want to waste my time. I wanted to rush to you; touch you; play with you; hug you; weep with you so I got up; went to the Common Hall and hanged myself.

CHAPTER TWENTY SIX

The Clouds of Mystery Scatter

My dead body was found in the Hall next morning. There was chaos everywhere. The school was closed; the students confined to their rooms. Not even a single bird was allowed to discuss the death issue.

The dead body was taken from the school secretly by my father's men. The lady warden investigated the case in the hostel. She came to know in a couple of days that Niharika was seen talking to me at the night before my suicide.

Ms. Vidhya took Niharika to task and punished her very severely. She was locked in a small room and not given food or water for many days. The weather changed drastically. There was heavy rain and snow fall here so the roads were blocked. No one was allowed to move to her room or render any sort of help. When the weather got clear, it had passed three days. My father visited the school and the room was unlocked to take the small girl out.

The girl had become a victim of the wrath of Nature and God. She was found dead lying on the floor. When taken to hospital, the doctor declared poison in her body. In fact she was bitten by a poisonous snake that entered her room to avoid rain.

It being a heavy rain and snow fall out, Wardens were confined to their rooms. No one bothered to take care of the little girl and left her hungry, thirsty, shivering from cold and fear to die weeping and sobbing in the room.

Niharika's father was a teacher. He filed a case against the school authorities for mismanagement, mishandling, corporal punishment and not informing the parents in the nick of time.

My father was quite powerful so he bribed the Police and got the case decided in his favor. There was a reign of terror and blood for months in the school.

Today I avenged Niharika's murder on the lady Warden—Vidhya —who left her to die in closed Horrors. She had committed suicide by hanging herself from a beam in the Building under construction.

She wiped her fevered brow and wore serene expressions.

Your Hillbilly is Radheshyam Kaka of our previous life. He is painfully aware of our wretched lives. He has seen both of us sitting, laughing and playing in his garden. We have plucked many flowers from his garden and made him angry, but he was always loving and caring. It was he who fetched a rose every night that I secretly put in your room.

An angelic smile ran across her lips. She looked smug when she resumed her speech.

I kept hovering all these years in this deserted place waiting for you. I was informed by a stroke of Fortune that one day you would meet me here only.

I can't show you the agony I have undergone in your wait. There was an uncomfortable silence in my life during all these years.

When you entered the School, I was very happy to see you after such a long time. This time you were a bit mature and taller comparatively. I had decided not to let you feel uncomfortable anyhow.

The laborer at the gate denied carrying your luggage so he became a victim of my wrath. He was very rude in his behavior. If anytime the students reached the Building under construction to take their ball, he used shout at them and scolded a lot. I could tolerate anything and everything but not any sort of impudence with you.

I wanted to teach him a lesson so I pushed him from the first floor. He got injured but his injuries were not so serious as to take his life. He died in the hospital for want of proper medical care. Your Froggy didn't want to pay for his medical expenses and the insurance money to the laborer so he bribed the doctor. The doctor injected him poison and he died. There was no one to claim for his death so the matter got appeased quickly.

"Do you want to see your Niharika of previous life?" She asked abruptly.

"Yes" I uttered unconsciously.

Your Birthday girl Deep Shikha is our Niharika of previous life.

She took a pause and resumed with a heart full of passion.

I visited the hostel daily to see you and cared for everyone who was in your touch. I never failed to visit the dormitory where you stayed when you had been a student here. I daily spent a few minutes there in perfect silence.

That day when I visited the hostel dormitory, all the students had gone to take refreshment. There was pin drop silence in dormitory. When I was returning, I saw a student sleeping soundly in his bed. You must have remembered the boy who fell in Dining Hall and started weeping. You reached the Hall and scolded the Head Cook for not serving the students properly.

Actually the same boy was left sleeping in bed by mistake. Since he was your affectionate, I sat down by his side in bed and caressed his hair. I woke him up and said to go for taking refreshment. When he rubbed the sleep from his eyes, I had gone.

Later on I came to know that he had got scared of me and hurt himself badly while breaking the panel of the door.

I felt very upset to see the little boy hurt and writhing in pain.

She looked sad and tears rolled down. She lifted her white fingers to collect the pearls and resumed.

I had many grievances against my father, but I never wanted to go against him. I saw him getting many illegal works done in collaboration with the Principal. When you were here, one occultist informed my father that you are Sarthak of previous life. This year I might do much harm to school property and could carry out my intentions against those who had harmed you. Taking his advice seriously and to avoid the dire consequences, my father made a plan to kill you in this life also. He sent two Bandicoots to throw you from the hill at the same place and to repeat the history. For the first time, I felt antipathy and hatred for my father in all these years. When you drove for the school in car, he ordered the Bandicoots to follow your car and throw it in the deep valley. My malignant reached to the extreme and I loosened the break shoe of his car. The car collided with a fast pacing car coming from opposite side because the driver failed to apply brakes and consequently he lost control over car.

I was sorry for his miserable death, but he deserved that kind of death only. His wickedness made him so hard that he took the life of a promising student like you, his own daughter who loved him more than anything in the world. Then again he tried to repeat his mistakes by throwing you in the mouth of Death.

Her face went panic-stricken and I read some expressions of horror on her face.

The Occultist with long mustaches sitting inside the Reception Hall knows everything about you and me. He has narrated everything to the Principal. That's why he has collected the Magicians and Exorcists from all over the place to catch my soul. All these psychics are busy carrying out a sort of exorcism. They want to send my soul to peace. How can I have peace without you by my side? I have wandered for 25 long years in search of you and now when my search is on the verge of completion, they want me to get away from you. But they are fools. Today, I'm quite powerful and can turn tables against their intentions. Today nothing will happen in their favor.

CHAPTER TWENTY SEVEN

An Incarnation of Innocence

Aanya is a very sweet, genial and congenial girl. Actually, she is my younger sister born of my father's second marriage, *but she doesn't know*. She also had an elder brother named Samar Pratap Singh who is in London. My father never scolded for her any mistake in life. Moreover, she never committed mistakes.

She is too innocent to be deceived or cheated. Don't take her otherwise. She is quite genuine in her feelings for you. It was me in her body that made love with you all the time. It was me who reached you all the times in your room. It was me who made love with you that night on the terrace.

Since the very first day of your arrival, I had decided to be a part of you all the time and feel the pleasure of your nearness. So I entered in her body and became a part and parcel of your love.

I felt disturbed to see both of you practicing dance together and then performing on the stage on the Teacher's Day. I felt unbearable when she embraced you, hugged you and became a good friend of yours on that day.

I could not share you with her. I felt hurt and decided to avenge myself. I disturbed her room and tried to throw her from the terrace. When you reached for her safety, I let her go.

But I could see the innocence on her face that proved her genuineness in friendship. She even doesn't know that she has slept with you many nights except the night of my assault. I realized my mistake and rearranged her room in proper order.

Tonight also she would have never accompanied you if she had not been possessed. It was me who was walking by your side.

Now I have relieved her. She is free. You can see her lying there in the garden under the bushes. She is unconscious but quite safe. She'll regain her consciousness after some time. She knows nothing about you and me. I thank her a lot, but now I don't need any one's help.

The warm tears full of emotions were still flowing from her big black eyes. She lifted her right hand. The bangles produced a heart appealing music. Wiping her tears, she gave me an amiable look full of emotions.

Sarthak, I have got you again. No one here can take you away from me now. I'll take you away from here so that no one can touch you or embrace you. I'll take you a place where the streams flow in all seasons; where the days never end; where lovers never get tired; where love never dies; where enemies of love can't reach; where the flowers never fade.

The love that I felt for you when you left me alone to die is still unrequited in my restless heart. It's beating extremely fast today feeling you so close to me. In a few moments I'll make you free from the shackles of life and then pour my limitless love on you. The tears I've shed in bygone years are asking for compensation. The heart wants to regain its normal speed. The eyes want to take a wink relief. I want to sleep peacefully in your lap forgetting the pain of parting.

She literally started shedding tears like anything.

Sarthak, her voice had got heavy I can't let you go now. I can't tolerate this world anymore. We'll run away from here, very far from human approaches. I'll never let you feel lonely. I'll take care of your every wish. We'll enjoy the sunrise in each other's embrace and never let the night shroud the moments of joy. Our world will become as beautiful as it was before.

She was all smiles again. She also smiled her thanks to me.

CHAPTER TWENTY EIGHT

An Albatross Around My Neck

She had narrated a painful incomplete story of boundless love in her heart. I was a mute listener of her long dramatic monologue. I was mesmerized; the tears were rolling down our cheeks. I felt sorry for both Aanya and Anushka. I had no memory of my previous birth so the conscience was not pricking and my heart had missed many beats. It was beating irregularly.

In the mean time, Froggy came rushing to me. He caught my hand, pulled me with all his might and dragged me out of the Garden. I was in a dilemma so responded him reluctantly. He could hardly manage to speak:

"Tanmay, you please run away from here. She wants to take you with her. I can stop her for a couple of seconds only. There is an Exorcist on the other side of the garden. Go to him. He'll make you understand how we can escape her wrath."

Next moment, he was hit hard on the head. The blood was pouring out of his head in buckets.

I was in a flux and turned to a stone. I spun around and a cold shiver of fear ran through me. A tremor of fear.

Anushka had gone violent with the interference of Froggy. She was striking him repeatedly on his head. I ran to the other side of the garden, crying and shouting for help. The awful din kept hitting my ears.

A tall man with long beard stopped and caught held my shoulder. I had seen that person in the Reception Hall practicing magic. He put a cross around my neck hurriedly; tied a black thread around my right arm another moment.

"Tanmay, I have circled this area with the power of magic. The cross around your neck and the sanctified thread will work as safety valve. She cannot harm you, but don't let her touch yourself otherwise she'll come to know about our plan." He regained his breaths and blurted, “Hide your cross under your shirt; go to her; coax her to come to this side and stand under this circle. Leave the rest on me. Her soul will get released and rest in peace. This is my promise. Now all is in your hands.”

I was split between my lost love of previous life and the words of the Exorcist to provide peace and rest to her wandering soul. Now I wanted to feel her at least once in the body of Aanya, but the fate didn’t seem grant my wish so I rushed to her. Froggy was lying on the grass and counting his last breaths. She was gazing at me. Her eyes were rolled up, but her face still had that glow and innocence that I felt on Aanya’s face every time.

“Be at peace. Don’t hurt him. Our love is innocent. We can’t take life of anyone.” I spoke consoling her.

Froggy’s clothes were ripped and shredded. Dark scratches covered his face and arms, and bright red blood tickled down his neck.

She had left Froggy to die and started stepping towards me. I retreated back slowly.

“Tanmay,” Froggy croaked weakly, barely able to talk. His last words melt my heart. And then he crumpled to the ground.

“Sir,” I cried in horror.

I dropped the little malice I had in my heart for him and ran to his side.

I knelt down beside him. “Are you okay?” I asked frantically.

His voice had gone silent. I pulled him up, but he had collapsed.

I spun to have a look at Anushka. She was all tears spreading her arms for a close hug.

“Sarthak,” Anushka said, “don’t run away from me. I’ll not harm you at all. I have loved you more than my breaths. You come with me; give me a warm embrace. I want to kiss you; sleep in your arms; have a few moments of perfect peace. In the last 25 years my eyes have not winked even once in your wait. They have turned into stone. They want to feel the warmth of your kisses. Don’t desert me. I can’t manage my life even a second more without you. I am tired.” *She kept speaking and I kept retreating.*

I had entered the circled area and she was standing at the outer circle. I wanted to invite her in so I raised my arms to embrace her.

The tears rolled down my eyes when I saw her crying in joy and rushing to me. I folded my arms and moved to aside. She was running after me laughing, enjoying playing. She looked perfectly happy waving her long white skirt that was kissing the ground. I wanted to turn and rush into her arms; squeeze her in my embrace;

kiss her lips, eyes and face all over. I stopped going away from her. I was fixed to ground. I wiped the rolling tears and gave way to sweet last smile to my lost love. She came rushing but stopped a few inches away. She took her arms back. She came to know that the Exorcist had put a cross around my neck and tied the sanctified thread on my arm. She retreated back. The smile on her face vanished replaced by gloom in eyes and then followed by a flood of tears. I had ripped her heart.

I had a look at the Exorcist. He gave me a signal so I rushed to his side weeping and leaving my love in lurch. I had deserted the love that had waited for me 25 long years; taken care of me all the time; made love with me and never let me feel lonely.

She also took a turn to get away from there, but the flames had engulfed her. I could hear the crackle of flames and feel the generating heat. She felt helpless, kept running on all the sides. The realization dawned upon her that she couldn't escape so stood in the middle of the Circle.

The Exorcist sprinkled a few drops of Holy Water on me and Aanya who was still unconscious, and kept chanting his deliverance prayers. I trusted his piety, prudence and personal integrity.

Anushka's eyes glowing brighter were full of love and affection for me. She was trapped in the fire. If she had been a human figure, I would have jumped in the fire and saved her, but I knew she must be relieved and her soul must rest in peace. I had loved her utmost in the previous life; she had been a part and parcel of my life in the last few months though unknowingly. Being her Love, I had a duty to get her soul exorcized.

The searing and blistering heat of the flames had started eating her outer self. She began crying out my name in pain.

"Sarthak, I know you'll not save me. You left me alone to die in this life also. I am fading away but I will be there for you always; I will wait for you in Heaven. Don't ever forget that I love you very much."

The red eyes glowed brighter in reaction to her screams. The fiery stare burnt into her eyes full of love, forcing me to shield my face with both hands.

My passions were running high. I rushed to her safety, but the way was blocked. I was held tightly by Daredevils.

"Let me go!" I screamed. "I have to save her! Move out of my way!"

The Exorcists kept exercising their mantras and paralyzed her. The crackle of flames grew to a roar. In a flash, she got converted into ashes. The sour odor choked me. I crashed on my elbow and knees and uttered a hurt cry. The darkness fell heavier and continued to wrap around me, holding me prisoner.

The pale crescent moon disappeared behind black wisps of cloud. The garden grew darker. The trees shook their leaves, sending whispers all around.

CHAPTER TWENTY NINE

Without Her I was Incomplete

The bright yellow glove was peeking through the lace curtain sending the mental and emotional turmoil of the night backstage. The lights of the day had chased away the shadow figures. I still had the heavy feeling of dread weighing me down, chilling my body. I felt wretched about the way things had turned out. Sadness descended upon me as I opened my eyes. Not since the death of my grandmother had I felt such a deadening gloom. May be not even then had I felt such a loss. The pain of departing from Anushka who sacrificed her life willingly for me was quite heavy on my heart. Deep down I still loved her whose love was forbidden for me.

In a couple of minutes, as a child I was surrounded by love and kindness of teachers—Rishabh, Abhi and others. Though they were not on the venue, they had been informed of the turbulence and upheaval caused at night.

Rishabh leaned over me, pulling the light blanket up to my chest. "How are you feeling now?" he asked softly.

I lay in bed, staring up at them, still feeling groggy and dazed. Abhi stood anxiously in the corner, his arms clasped tensely in front of him, looking on in silence. I could read his lips and feel the tears lurking in the corners of his big eyes.

I beckoned Abhi closer and brushed the tears off his cheeks.

"I—I'm okay." I said, pulling myself up a bit on the pillow. "I'm just a little exhausted."

I felt a shiver to see the Exorcist, a tall man with white beard, entering my room followed by a handsome boy. The new face was Mr. Samar Pratap Singh, son of the Owner of the school. He had a feeling of gloom and depression in his eyes. Seeing them, the teachers left the room. I raised my head and sat against the wall with the support of the pillow. We sat in gloomy silence; the boy on the sofa and the Exorcist on the edge of my bed.

"How are you feeling now after the night's fitful fever?" the Exorcist asked me.

"I am fine, but the sense of guilt is quite heavy on my heart." I moaned getting restless.

He asked me to remove the cross from my neck and untie the black thread. They were sanctified for a particular reason. I followed his instructions. He made me wear another cross that he blessed with silent prayers.

The young man reached my bed and held my hands tightly. The tears rolled down his cheeks. "I am Aanya's younger brother. I was born and bred in London. I never saw Anushka, my elder sister, but heard that she had an unconditional love for you. Now when she is no more, I request you as a brother of your Lost Love to offer her ashes to the sacred Ganges at Kashi and do the Shradh. Her soul will really feel relieved to have Death Rituals by your hands."

I felt like saying something, but the words caught in my throat. I was surprised by the wave of emotion that swept over me.

I also wanted her ashes to be scattered at Ganges in Kashi so we proceeded to collect the ashes in the gathering gloom of the winter's afternoon.

When I looked at the broad misty lawn and at the garden of withered flowers along the fence, her sweet little face got reflected. I dropped on my knees to embrace her ashes. The breeze seemed carrying the echo of her voice.

"I will be there for you always; I will wait for you in Heaven. Don't ever forget that I love you very much . . .."

The cheeks went wet with tears. I had collected her in a small urn to be carried to Kashi, my education place. The urn was kept at the Reception Hall where the Holy men performed certain rituals.

The time interval I spent signing my Resignation, and packing my luggage that was assisted by Chirag and other Daredevils. The car was ready to drop me. I left my room behind with a heavy heart; handed the keys to Rishabh. I had a last wish to see Aanya, but turned down the idea at the thought of making her sad.

The love of Anushka was more than enough to spend this life happily so I hurried down to the Reception Hall. The students from girls and boys hostel had collected to see me off. The luster of their innocent faces seemed fading away. They had come with Autograph Diaries that they held against their chests. When I reached them, they raised their Diaries. I shared my love with the little buds.

When I turned, I heard a sweet voice.

Tussi ja rahe ho?

I turned. It was no other than Birthday girl, Niharika of my previous life. I lifted her in my arms; pasted many caresses on her cheeks and forehead; signed her Diary and dropped her down with glum in my eyes.

I was taken to surprise by Aanya standing near the car and waiting for me.

"Hi! I never expected that you'll meet me here. I thought you would be sleeping." I said holding on my grim.

"What had you thought? You would go away without me. I am not going to leave you so easily. I am going to Kashi with you." She said with a wry smile.

To my utter astonishment, Mr. Samar stepped towards me; place his right hand on my left shoulder and spoke:

"I'm sorry Tanmay. I couldn't deny her. My father loved her most in the world. I can't hurt his feelings. She must be with you sharing all the rituals at Kashi. Don't deny, please." When he had finished, his voice got heavy.

"Bye. Take care." He started to sob uncontrollably and walked away.

CHAPTER THIRTY

I'll Wait for You

The violent storm consuming passion had gone calm. The luster of the life had been turned into ashes. All other issues had faded into insignificance. The sky held no fascination. My words had lost the power to charm. The boyish charm had faded away from the agonized face. The blowing strong puffs were blocking the way and pushing backward.

Two grim faces had reached the religious capital of our country to dispose of the ashes of my Anushka in the holy river Ganges. There was a feeling of restlessness deep in my soul. Her reminiscence laid heavy on my conscience.

The early morning at Ghats was grim. Despair hanged heavy in the stifling air. A dull monotony was prevailing over the sleeping boatmen on the stairs. The rising sun was lethargic in lightning the world. The breeze was carrying an unpleasant music. The irregular waves in the Ganges were reciting the dirges for the bodies waiting for cremation. The hungry birds were flying in search of foodgrains.

We had reached the bank of Ganges with a belief that those who die out of Kashi, cremation on the banks of the Ganges or the disposing of the ashes in her waters is the most suitable thing.

We hired a priest who carried out the death rituals at the bank to offer contentment to the departed soul, and promote comfort and happiness for successors.

He prepared some *pinda*, round balls of rice and flour; sprinkled the holy water and chanted mantras. He offered it to the cow, the fish in Ganges and crows that are considered a connection between the world of the living and the world of the dead. Then the food was offered to Brahmins.

The Brahmins conducted *Tarpan*, offering of water to the deceased. They added milk, oats, rice, sesame seeds, sandalwood and flowers as custom when tarpan ritual took place. The mixture was offered in a small stream made with the use of *kusha* and offered while chanting mantras.

"When this offering is made with devotion, gratitude, goodwill, love and good wishes, it immediately ensures contentment for the departed soul." The priest suggested.

Then I stepped in the Ganges till the water reached above my knees. The heart gave a hard beat and I couldn't store the courage to dispose of the ashes. It had the love of my previous and present life. I thought of rubbing my love all around my body and pass my whole life with her. Her sweet little face got reflected and voice reverberated,

"Sarthak, drop me from your hands. This world is too cruel to respect love. I bear you no grudge.... I bid you good bye....I will be there for you always; I'll wait for you in Heaven. Don't ever forget that I love you beyond human limits."

Then she vanished before the eyes of my mind. She was the soul of discretion. I opened my eyes to the reality of world. She wished herself a million miles away. I concluded the earthly sojourn of her afflicted soul by mixing the ashes of my living soul in the sacred water of auspicious Ganges along with garlands and flowers to send it to Heaven where she had been waiting for me.

"Anushka, I feel our love was impossible. But I wish we could turn the clock years back and give our forbidden love another chance." I gave way to suppressed agony, but it was no use wishing for the impossible.

The bitter disappointment streamed down from my cheeks lighting the chilled water of the river.

I waved final bye-bye to the ashes flowing with the waves; took a turn and walked away holding Aanya's hand without looking back.

All was dispersed by the morning breeze; the lines on the face had washed away. She came from dust, and that's what life turned her into. We were drenched in our tears, and silently kept fading away; the souls were in anguish.

If Life is so cruel, what good we can expect from Death?

If Laughter steals joy of soul, what good we can expect from tears?

If Meeting has so much pain, what good we expect from Parting?

If Love had to exit like this, why make an entry of these sighs?

If the sweet memories are so blistering, what good we expect from Cursed?

If the dreams are nightmares, what good we expect from Night?

If I had won my love, what was that I had lost in Ganges?
If it is life, how much better be death?"

I stopped on my way, looked at my Aanya and moved on.

Let these dreams flow in Ganges, open your eyes to the morrow.
Burry the issues of yesterday, hold tight the time of tomorrow.
We seem to have all, but nothing really;
Halt is part of life like moving ahead.

Let these bitter memories flow from your eyes, hold sweet ones tight in mind."

(***Life stops, but Love prevails***)